THE DEVIL'S DEACON

Floyd T. Goad was paid by the railroad to hunt down those who held up their trains and robbed the passengers. Right now, he was after the man who dynamited Forty-Mile Cutting. Posing as a quack pill doctor, he was sent on the trail of the dynamiters, but deadly knives and hot lead faced him and it was in the lap of the gods whether he could accomplish his dangerous mission.

D1502455

THE DEVIL'S DEACON

by

Elliot Conway

Dales Large Print Books
Long Preston, North Yorkshire,
BD23 4ND, England.

British Library Cataloguing in Publication Data.

Conway, Elliot
        The devil s deacon.

        A catalogue record of this book is
        available from the British Library

        ISBN   1-84137-020-7 pbk

First published in Great Britain by Robert Hale Ltd., 1999

Copyright ' 1999 by Elliot Conway

Cover illustration ' Faba by arrangement with Norma Editorial
S.A.

The right of Elliot Conway to be identified as the author of this
work has been asserted by him in accordance with the
Copyright, Designs and Patents Act, 1988

Published in Large Print 2000 by arrangement with Robert Hale
Ltd.

Dales Large Print is an imprint of Library Magna Books Ltd.

Printed and bound in Great Britain by
T.J. (International) Ltd., Cornwall, PL28 8RW

For Colin and Rita Watson

One

'Get the boys from the cutting, Murphy!' Spenser, the track superintendent yelled. 'The supply train's coming in with the gear we're waiting for!'

Along with the lengths of rail track, wooden ties, fishplates, with which the flatbeds had been loaded at the depot in Abilene, Spenser hoped that they hadn't forgotten to send the barrels of beer he had promised his construction crew for clearing the way for the tracks to be laid through Forty-Mile cutting ahead of schedule. The cutting was the last major engineering problem on the sixty-mile spur line of the Atchinson, Topeka, Sante Fe railroad that ran from Abilene, Kansas, south to Newton.

Spenser reckoned that his Irish diggers wouldn't need any more incentives to work like horses laying the rest of the iron road to Newton. The prospects of spending their pay, and the bonuses, in the gin palaces and bawdyhouses that Newton boasted, was all the encouragement they needed.

Spenser waited at the side of the track till the loco had drawn up, hissing steam, bell clanging, at the huddle of tents that marked the end-of-track camp, then he walked along the line to check the loads on the rail cars. He was pleased to see the two rifle-armed guards on each of the three flatbeds.

The work on laying the spur line hadn't only been hampered by the terrain. Twice, loose rails had caused a derailment of the weekly supply train. A trestle bridge over a wash collapsed for no apparent reason, sudden rock slips blocking the tracks. All unexplained 'accidents'. Spenser had been laying tracks for the Kansas Pacific for over twelve years, his bridges didn't fall down, or rails jump loose on their ties. While the general feeling at head office was that the accidents were just the average run of bad luck any major construction work would suffer, they had to take the views of the chief line superintendent seriously, that what he built stayed built. So, extra guards were posted on every supply train that ran to the end-of-line camp.

'We've brung the beer you asked for, Mr Spenser!' one of the guards on the first flatbed shouted. 'We were thinkin' of haulin' out some of Poker Alice's short-time girls for your Micks as a treat.'

Spenser grinned. 'I make 'em sweat, not some young whore.' Then, face serious again, he said, 'Did you have a clear run down?'

'Yeah,' replied the guard. 'Everything was OK. We checked out every bridge before the train crossed ... what the hell!' He gasped as the sound of an explosion vibrated along the iron rails.

Spenser looked along the tracks at the rising cloud of dust. His face twisted in anger. 'Some sonuvabitch has dynamited the cutting!' he cried. 'You and your buddy,' he said to the guard, 'get on to that ridge and shoot anyone you see skulking around up there.' Then, raising his voice, he yelled, 'The rest of you boys come with me, my crew's working in that cutting!'

The rescue party met the survivors stumbling, coughing, choking, out of the thick curtain of dust. Later when they brought out the dead Spenser thought, grimly, that they might move ass at Abilene and get someone down here pronto, to try and catch the bastards responsible for the *accidents*.

Two

Silas Black, the regional manager of the Kansas Pacific Railroad Company, close-eyed the man sitting on the other side of his desk. He'd had no call on Mr Floyd Goad's services before so somehow the big, running-to-seed, heavily-jowled man, dressed soberly in a preacher's black broad-cloth – he even had the unctuous smile of a sky-pilot – didn't seem to fit with his record as the KP's number-one regulator.

Then, gazing even closer at his visitor, Silas saw that the fat man's oily smile didn't extend to his eyes. Silas shivered involuntarily under the cold-eyed piercing gaze. Then he well believed that Mr Goad's sobriquet of the Devil's Deacon, earned by dispatching numerous bad-asses who had tried to rob the KP trains to stoke up the

11

fires of Hell, was no exaggeration but fully justified.

'I suppose head office has briefed you about the trouble we're having on the new spur line, Mr Goad?' he said.

Mr Floyd Goad nodded, his smile vanishing.

'At first, I thought all the mishaps were genuine accidents,' Silas continued. 'Until the explosion at the cutting that cost the lives of four of the construction crew. I owed Mr Spenser, the line boss, an apology for doubting his word that the loose rails, the collapsed bridges weren't accidents. Of course, I'll give you all the help you ask for, and the local law is out looking for leads on the dynamiters.'

'It seems that someone doesn't want the spur line built, Mr Black,' Floyd said. 'Someone with a whole heap of money to be able to hire men to pull down bridges and blow up cuttin's. So that don't mean a disgruntled employer.' Floyd twisted ass in his chair so that he was looking out of one of the office windows. 'M'be someone like the boss of the Abilene/Newton freight line whose premises I can see across the street there.'

Silas Black laughed. 'You can't be serious, Mr Goad.' He said: 'Why, Turner Lazenby, who owns the line, is a respected member of the town's business community, could be our next mayor. His company does some contract work for us.'

Floyd swung back and faced Silas Black again. Flat-voiced, he said, 'His freight line won't be haulin' much freight between Abilene and Newton once the tracks get through to Newton, will it? Lawbreakers come in all shapes and sizes, Mr Black. Some are two-gun stomping men, some are hard-faced businessmen. They're the toughest kind to root out with enough proof to convict them in a court of law.'

Silas got the shakes once more as Mr Goad's penetrating gaze cut into him again. He thought he saw the big man's lip twist in what could be a shadowy smile. God, he thought, panicky, did the smooth-faced son-of-a-bitch know that he was humping the mayor's wife? Then the big man got to his feet and Silas guessed that it was Mr Goad's chilling, assaying looks that had stirred a guilty conscience in him. Never again would he judge a man at first appearance.

'Thanks for your offer of help, Mr Black,' Floyd said. 'But I figure that the fella who's causing this trouble on the line will know that the KP will be sending an investigator here.' He showed a mouthful of white tombstone teeth in a smile as icy as his gaze had been. 'I don't intend givin' him the edge of him knowin' me before I find out who he is.' Floyd tipped his hat in a farewell gesture. 'I'll sneak out the way I snuck in, and I'd be obliged if you would keep our meetin' secret. One of your staff could loose-mouth off in some bar about me bein' here. Let's keep the fella we're huntin' guessin' what the railroad's plans are to stop any more damage bein' done to the line. It could get him worried, m'be make the bastard careless.'

Silas Black got up from his chair. 'I'll do my part, Mr Goad. Extra guards are being posted on the supply trains, and armed men are now stationed at the end-of-line camp. All have got orders to shoot on sight anyone acting suspiciously near the tracks.' He leaned across his desk and shook Floyd's hand with a firm grip, and glimpsed the big pistol poking out of a holster under the big man's left shoulder, and another gun showing above the top of his pants. The two guns didn't seem to be in keeping with the sober garb of Mr 'Deacon' Goad.

Floyd, noticing the railroad manager's surprised look, gave him another all-toothed grin and flicked his right wrist.

'Well I'll be damned!' Silas gasped, sitting back down in his chair, his wide-eyed gaze fixed on the small, snub-nosed pistol nestling in the palm of Floyd's hand.

'Someone once said, so I've been led to believe,' Floyd said, 'that the pen is mightier than the sword.' He gave a loud, derisory snort. 'Whoever that *hombre* was, Mr Black, he sure didn't live west of the Mississippi. Most of the hard men who rob and kill out here can't damn well write. Even if they could scribe they know that a Colt or a Winchester shell carries more weight in a dispute than a whole passel of books.' Floyd slipped the derringer back into its clip. 'I'll be about my business now, Mr Black. I'll let you know, if I can, of any progress I make.' He favoured Silas with another fearsome grin before turning and striding out of the room. And Silas Black discovered something else about Mr Floyd Goad: for all his bulk the regulator could move as silently as a shadow.

A thoughtful Silas sat in his chair for a while after Floyd had left. He knew that Goad had a first-class rep as a trouble-shooter but in this case he was convinced that the big man was starting off his investigation on the wrong foot if he was suspecting that Turner Lazenby could be somehow involved with the dynamiters.

He opined that the man, or men, who

were responsible for the trouble on the spur line, would be disgruntled sodbusters on whom the railroad had put pressure to sell their strips of dirt for give-away prices. Although a loyal servant of the company, Silas had to admit that in the building of the Sante Fe line the Kansas Pacific had ridden roughshod over a lot of the farmers, illegally roughshod at times.

Floyd slipped out of the side alley to stand at its opening surveying Main Street, Abilene. In a quick, but calculating glance, he counted fifteen saloons and gin parlours. Coming into town from south of the KP tracks, he had passed at least ten herds waiting to be driven into the stockyards, the last leg of their long trek from Texas on the hoof. Apart from the herd riders, most of the drovers would be frequenting the saloons and cathouses in town. Then later, whooping it up, cutting loose with their big pistols at any target that took their drunken fancy. Abilene, he could see, was a wide-open burg. It had to be to keep the hard-riding, hard-drinking Texans happy. The town would also attract the conmen, the tinhorn gamblers and the bad-asses. Plenty of candidates for the man who was disrupting the building of the spur line to pick from, if the price suited them. So it wouldn't be easy to find the dynamiters. Floyd shrugged his shoulders; whenever was it easy to track down lawbreakers?

He hadn't to forget that as well as not being easy, hunting killers was also downright dangerous. Whoever was at the back of the dynamiting would be expecting the KP to pull out all the stops to seek him out. And if he could have construction workers killed in the furtherance of his schemes, he wouldn't hesitate in having a railroad agent shot down if he felt him a threat to his wellbeing. To counter that threat he had taken precautions to prevent him from being buried in an early grave on Boot Hill.

Floyd grinned as he looked across the street at the gaudily painted box-wagon hitched to a big lantern-jawed, mottled-hide mule. Sign written across the wagon's sides was the slogan, 'Genuine Indian Potions and Medicines. Guaranteed cures for, Baldness, Aching Joints, Coughing Sickness and Lack of Manliness'. Underneath, in somewhat smaller script, came, 'Doctor Floyd T. Goad, late of Harvard Medical Faculty'.

A quack doctor and pill pedlar could be in no way tagged as a railroad investigator. It had worked on other assignments. If it did go wrong on this occasion, Floyd knew he wouldn't have much time to wonder why his cover had been blown: he would be dead, pronto-like.

He got up on to the wagon seat, heeled off the brake as he tugged on the reins and with a cry of 'Move ass, Ulysses!' the wagon jerked forward along Main Street, its contents rattling noisily inside, to the livery barn. Floyd glanced casually at the name sign above the door on the saloon next to the compound of the Abilene/Newton freight line. Its owner was the man Silas Black had told him was boss of the freight line, and pillar of the community. Floyd's nose twitched like a mountain lion smelling its next meal. Turner Lazenby, he thought, had more to lose than the dropping off of his freight business to Newton if the line went through. He would also miss out on the Texas trail-hands' pay ringing the bells of the tills in his saloon.

The man who was causing all the disruption on the line wasn't doing it for the kicks and in spite of Silas Black's speaking-up for Lazenby he knew that even well-respected citizens, when they see their high-living style of life going down the drain, sometimes act like out-and-out desper-adoes. Floyd was getting a gut-feeling that it hadn't been just a wild guess naming Turner Lazenby as a man whose interests would be better served if the line wasn't built. He now had, he judged, a possible suspect. It would pay him to have a closer look at the freight-owner's activities. See if he had contact with men who, he opined, weren't too fussy how they earned their due. It wasn't much of a lead but it was a start in his investigation.

Poker Alice, madam of the Smoky Hills bordello, looked down from her first-floor veranda at the painted wagon rattling over the sun-baked hard ruts of what passed for a street south of the tracks in Abilene. She smiled. Her clients didn't need pills to improve their manliness; the Texas horn-dogs wanted something to cool them down.

She saw the big, heavy-built man driving the wagon raise his hat in greeting to her. It would be a pity, Poker Alice thought, if such a fine figure of a man ended up being run out of town, bare-assed naked, all tarred and feathered, roped to a length of split-rail fencing. That's what the Texans would do to him if he tried to con them out of their hard-earned pay with his fake medicines. She raised her hand in an acknowledging wave and got back the full-faced smile of a man who had just stepped off the train from Hicksville, with straw sticking out of his ears. Or, Poker Alice thought, the skin-deep mask of a man who was a smooth operator, and reckoned that the trail-hands had better hold real tight to their hard-earned dollars.

It wasn't a dimwit's eyes that were taking in the madam's heavy, creamy-white breasts, practically all on show when her wrap flapped open as she waved to him. Floyd shook his head to clear it of the lewd thoughts he was feeling towards the plump-figured woman. Business before pleasure, he told himself, especially a business that could turn into a killing spree. Sighing deeply, he tugged the left-hand rein and the wagon turned into the livery-barn yard.

Three

Turner Lazenby was standing drinking a glass of his special Scotch in the Prairie Dog saloon, his saloon, reviewing the efforts he had taken to discourage the building of the Newton spur line. He would keep up the damaging raids on the line till the Kansas Pacific decided that it was proving too expensive to build. He was well aware that the killing of the track workers at the cutting would have raised the stakes against him and the dynamiters somewhat.

Investigators would soon be ranging around the territory looking for the where-abouts of the line wreckers and anyone connected with them, but he was willing to accept that risk. If the line south to Newton was completed he would lose the lucrative business his freight line brought in hauling supplies to Newton. And he could kiss goodbye to the Texas trail-hands drinking his high-priced rotgut-whisky in his bar. In short he would go bust.

It wasn't fair, Lazenby thought bitterly, as he took another pull at his single malt. He had sweated his balls off building up his business. Risked his life more times than he could remember hauling stores to outlying farms and ranches when the whole god-damned territory was being quartered by Comanche warbands out on killing and cutting-out raids. He wasn't against progress; he knew the railroad was here to stay, and would expand its tracks. All he wanted was for it not to grow too fast, not till he had made his fortune.

To ease his worries somewhat, Lazenby decided to have a word with Mort Behen, a man whom he regularly employed as a wagon-train guard, the man he was paying extra to dissuade the Kansas Pacific from laying their track to Newton. He hadn't been in contact with him since the dynamiting of the cutting and wanted to make sure that Behen hadn't left any sign there that could lead the law to him. He was banking on it, risking putting his own neck in the noose no less, that Behen, an ex-Missouri brush boy, was an adept hand at covering his backtrail.

He paid Behen well for his sabotaging of the line, but he knew that no amount of hard cash bought loyalty from characters like Behen. If things went sour for the Missourian, to save his miserable hide the dirty son-of-a-bitch wouldn't hesitate to finger him as the man who was paying for the raiding. Lazenby shivered. The killings at the cutting would brand him as a murderer alongside Behen. He ran a trembling finger round the inside of his collar. He could feel the hemp tightening around his neck. But he was in too deep to back out of his grand plan to keep his business in the black. He downed the rest of his drink and walked out of the saloon, heading for Poker Alice's cathouse.

He had to go there to escort Poker Alice to

her weekly game of poker held here in the saloon. It would give him a chance to talk to Behen. He would be there, raising a sweat, or cooling off from a heavy session with one of Poker Alice's girls.

Poker Alice saw Turner Lazenby hurrying along the street towards her place. He was early if he was just coming to take her to the card game, she wasn't ready yet. Poker Alice's heart began to beat faster. Maybe, she thought, Turner had the notion to bounce her around her well-sprung bed before the poker game. The big, wide-smiling pill pedlar had surprisingly stirred up her blood.

She hurried back inside, quickly dabbed a few drops of her expensive genuine Paris, France, perfume behind her ears and other tantalizing places, before posturing herself on her bed, wrap revealingly open, there to wait, eager and impatient, for Turner's rapping on her door. Twenty minutes later she was still waiting, cursing most unlady-like, her angry disappointment rapidly cooling her sudden passionate urges.

'Damnit, where the hell is Turner?' she exclaimed savagely. Ashamed with herself for acting like a young bride on her wedding waiting for her husband to join her in bed, towards a man to whom – if they had both been thirty years younger – she wouldn't have given a second look. She got up from the bed and stepped out and looked down into the lounge. Several customers were sitting there chatting to the girls before bringing them up into the private rooms. She saw Turner in deep conversation with Mort Behen. She knew that Behen, and the men who rode with him, hired themselves out to Turner's freight company. Personally, she wouldn't give the weasel-eyed son-of-a-bitch, Behen, the time of day.

She could do without Behen's cash. She would have barred him from coming into her place and roughing up the girls when drunk if she hadn't known that Behen had an unsavoury rep of being a hair-triggered killing man. It wouldn't have been right to get her bouncers to risk their lives trying to throw him out.

It must be urgent business Turner was discussing with Behen, Poker Alice thought, for him to buttonhole him here in the sporting house instead of at his office. And serious by the worried look Turner was wearing. Though all the businessmen in Abilene weren't exactly jumping with joy at the prospect of the spur line being built, making Newton the up-and-coming rail-head cattle town in Kansas and turning Abilene into a ghost town.

She had seen the writing on the barn door and had bought property in Newton. She would move her girls and furniture there. She would soon establish herself. The girls would be catering for their old and regular customers, two, three weeks earlier. Turner, Poker Alice opined, would have to go into a new line of business. Turner saw her standing there and broke off his conversation with Behen and came across to the stairs. She gave a wry smile as she re-entered her room. Turner sure didn't appear as though he had fun and games on his mind. Life, as she well knew, and as Turner seemed to have just found out, wasn't always a bowl of cherries.

Behen gave a sneering grin as he watched Lazenby walking up the stairs. He had smelt the sweat of fear and panic on the freight-owner when he was talking to him. These soft-assed businessmen were all the same. They wanted to make money, but when the going got dirty and blood had to be spilt, their yellow streak began to show.

'Make one more raid against the line, a good one,' Lazenby had told him. 'Things are getting too hot to risk any more than that.'

Risk? That was good, thought Behen, sarcastically. He and his boys were doing all the risking. He didn't have to be told that it was going to be more dangerous attacking the line now, that's why he had asked Lazenby to raise the ante on the next raid, and Lazenby had willingly paid it.

The town marshal had men out looking for their tracks and the railroad had posted extra guards along the line and on the supply train. They were the problems he could see and get over; they couldn't watch every yard of the track. What was causing Behen unease was where were the Kansas Pacific's own investigators, the Pinkertons, whom the railroad must have brought in, the men who worked undercover? They must be in Abilene now doing their snooping around. His boys had been hanging around the rail depot these past few days watching for any man getting off the train who had the look of a law-enforcer about him. He was taking a stroll around the saloons, keeping his ears open for anyone asking questions about the raid.

Behen judged it to be lying-low time. When things quietened down he would hit the line again, unexpectedly, good and hard.

Four

Floyd had seen Ulysses fed and watered, his wagon – his sleeping quarters – safely parked in the livery barn compound, and was now walking back to the saloon section of the town, the Prairie Dog saloon in particular. He intended giving out the leaflets he had stuffed in his pockets advertising his healing presence in town to the bar's customers hoping it would give him a chance to close-eye Mr Lazenby Turner to professionally weigh him up to see if the freight-owner was as upright and honest a citizen as Silas Black swore he was.

An Indian medicine-man would call it 'smelling out'. He'd settle for calling it playing a hunch, an old lawman's gut-feeling. A way-out hunch, Floyd had to admit, but he had to start off the investigation somewhere and right now Turner Lazenby, a man with a more pressing need than most in Abilene not to want the spur line put through, seemed the right man to check out first.

Young Joshua Webb stepped off the boardwalk and on to the street to walk round the four trail-hands who were deliberately blocking his way in front of the general store. He could see by the way they were swaying on their feet that they were liquored up and on the prod. He proved himself frighteningly right when the biggest of the four, a scowling-faced, glowering-eyed man who dwarfed him in height and weight stepped on to the street and stood in his way.

'Well lookee here, boys,' he said, grinning wolfishly, 'a sonuvabitch blue-belly.'

Joshua's bloodcount rose in anger. It was his pa's tunic, still showing proudly, the faded marks of a sergeant's chevrons.

'Have yuh got the balls tuh yank out that hogleg yuh're totin', Nigra lover?' he heard the big Texan say. 'Or are yuh yaller like all you Yankees?'

Joshua ran a dry tongue over dryer lips as he cast a nervous look at the four Texans. He had balls all right, the reb sons-of-bitches were holding him tight by them. Though he had been too young to have fought under the 'Bonny Blue Flag'. His pa had called the Southern guerrillas murdering, bushwhacking sons-of-bitches, a disgrace to the Rebel cause. His pa's farm had been on the Missouri side of the Kansas/Missouri border. The wrong side for a man who favoured Abe Lincoln and the Union.

He was now mad enough to throw down on the big ape if he didn't know that his pa's ancient cap and ball Walker, sheathed in a flapped cavalry holster about his belly, often misfired. He also knew that if he could beat the big Texan to the draw his buddies would cut loose at him. He was dead if he didn't pull out his gun and he could be heading for Boot Hill if he did. Josh bit the bullet.

'I take it you're man enough to let me loose the flap on my holster, mister?' he said, in a voice that belied his inner fear. 'Or you might as well plug me where I stand. I ain't drawin' against a man with an open holster.'

Floyd walked round the corner and took in the whole scene with one fleeting glance. He had come to Abilene undercover, getting himself involved in a gunfight would draw unwelcome attention to himself, or shot dead. Yet he couldn't let the kid be gunned down like a dog, a Union kid at that.

'You do that, pilgrim,' Floyd said. 'Give the kid an even break.' The four Texans spun round. Hands reaching for pistols stayed as they saw that the unexpected interruption to their fun was holding two pistols on them.

'These two beauties,' continued Floyd, 'will make sure that you three *hombres* don't try and swing the odds in your *compadre*'s favour.' The Texans heard the ominous clicks of the hammers of the Colts covering them being thumbed back. Floyd nodded to the kid. 'OK, boy, make your play; it's a fair fight now.'

The Texan's pistol cleared leather first, though a liquor-fuddled brain made his aim unsteady, and lost him his edge. Surprisingly cool, Joshua heard the shell hum past his left ear, then his own gun was in his hand, and with his arm fully extended, as though about to shoot a can off a fence, he squeezed the trigger, praying hard that the Walker wouldn't let him down or he would be dead before the next shell came under the hammer.

The Walker boomed and flamed and Joshua saw the Texan recoil a few paces as the shell struck him. Where he had hit him, Joshua couldn't tell, but he hadn't just winged him for the Texan, groaning loudly, had dropped to his knees and fell forward on to his face. Panic brought the acidity rushing up to the back of Joshua's throat. Had he killed the Texan? Could he be charged with murder? He almost cried with relief when he saw the Texan's legs twitching, though his groans were now only sobbing moans. The sound of another shot made him jump and he saw one of the other three Texans clutching at his right shoulder, then heard his unknown ally say, 'I told you boys to stay out of the fight, didn't I? Anyone else foolish enough to go for his gun I'll plug between the eyes, *comprende?* The fight is over, kid, so put your gun up and we'll leave these *hombres* to see to their wounded.'

Floyd held the pistols on the Texans till Joshua had joined him. Then, out of the side of his mouth he hissed, 'I'd get up on to your horse, kid, and ass-kick it outa town, *pronto*. Every Texan in town will be out for your blood once these spread the word around what's happened here.'

'I ain't got a horse, mister,' replied Joshua.

Floyd cursed. He had risked unwanted attention only to prolong the kid's life for a few hours. 'What the hell happened to your horse?' he snarled.

'I had to sell it,' Joshua said. 'Or I'd be sleepin' and eatin' in some hogpen or other.'

Floyd gave a surly grunt of understanding and did some rapid thinking before he said, 'You'd better latch on to me, kid, till this trouble blows over. Go and pick up what gear you've still got and meet me at the livery barn; make it quick.' He switched his full attention back on to the Texans. He saw no more trouble coming from them. The two unwounded trail-hands had their hands full picking up their badly wounded *compadre*. Though he did get some dirty-mouthing from the man he had winged and the shouted threat of, 'You and the kid are dead, dead! The rest of the crew will see to that!'

Floyd T. Goad, he told himself, on the way to the livery barn, you've sure made one helluva balls-up of this investigation. He now couldn't stroll casually into the Prairie Dog saloon to weigh up his one and only suspect, Mr Turner Lazenby, in case he met up with the rest of the Texans and got himself shot full of holes. Although his original plan was too risky to carry out he wasn't about to sit on his ass in the wagon doing damn all till the Texans left town. After all, he was supposed to be the Kansas/Pacific's number-one investigator. His pride was at stake.

His alternative plan, just thought up, to keep the investigation rolling, was to make the trip to the end-of-track camp. Peddle his pills, and do a little scouting around to try and cut sign at the cutting. The dynamiters must have been up on horses, they hadn't flown there. Maybe, he thought, gloomily, if there were tracks they would give him an idea of how many men he was hunting and, if real lucky, where they were heading for. The middle of nowhere, he reckoned the way his luck was running.

Floyd ceased thinking about his plan because the more he did so the more it seemed like no plan at all. At least, he tried to convince himself, he was starting to earn his pay.

Now it all depended on the kid. It would be a long haul for one man up on the wagon seat and Ulysses wasn't exactly the most sweet-tempered and co-operative of mules. If the kid was stony broke he'd probably be glad to grab the chance of being a mule-skinner for a spell. Floyd smiled. He hoped the kid could swear and curse. Ulysses needed to be shown who was boss.

Five

The sweat stuck Joshua's shirt and pants to his body. His arms and back ached with the strain of tugging at the rein to hold the mule on to the trail. The four-legged son-of-Satan wanted to wander where the hell took his fancy, threatening to overturn the wagon. Joshua wondered why he hadn't just bundled up his gear and lit out for Missouri on foot instead of working for Mr Goad for a week or two till the Texans had quit Abilene. Or shot the blamed mule and hauled the wagon himself. He would have raised less sweat that was for sure.

Floyd, dozing on the seat alongside him, raised one eyelid, lips twitching slightly in a smile as he heard the kid cursing at Ulysses. He didn't know that a young Missourian dirt-farmboy was familiar with such a string of curse words.

Joshua cast another you've-dropped-me-in-it, glance at Floyd and tried once more to assay him. If he hadn't seen him in action against the trail-hands, handling two pistols as though he had cut his teeth on them, he would have taken the smooth-smiling Mr Goad in his black store suit as a circuit stump preacher, or a forked-tongued lawyer. And the alertness he had seen in the big man's eyes as he continually watched the trail when he was driving the wagon out of Abilene he knew for certain that his new boss wasn't only a seller of patent medicines and pills. The look reminded him of the steely-eyed gazes of the two-gun border *pistoleros* he had read about in Ned Buntline's *Tales of the Untamed Frontier.*

So, just who the hell was Mr Floyd T. Goad, he asked himself? There was a big solid chest, heavily padlocked, in the back of the wagon. It would be full of guns and whisky for trading with some Comanche warband. A trade that was a hanging offence. While he was beholden to Mr Goad, that didn't mean hanging under a tree alongside him. He tugged hard at the reins and brought the wagon to a sudden shuddering halt. He screwed round on the seat and eyeballed Floyd.

'Mr Goad,' he said. 'It ain't that I'm not grateful at you pulling me out of a hairy situation back there in town, and you taking me on when I'm flat broke, but it's only fittin' that I know what I'm letting myself in for workin' for you.'

Floyd raised his eyebrows in surprise. Then he smiled at Joshua. 'In for, boy? Why, you're in for bein' my driver and we're headin' to the camp to sell my pills and such-like to the wild Irish boys workin' on the track there.'

'Don't give me that pill-peddlin' crap, Mr Goad!' Joshua said angrily. 'I may be just a farmboy but I ain't completely dumb. You ain't a doctor of medicine as it states on the side of this wagon here, even though you've got it full of pills. My guess is you ain't a doctor of anything. And you sure ain't a badge-toting lawman, not wearing that fancy shoulder holster.' Joshua's face hardened. 'I reckon you're a no-good renegade and you're meeting up with a bunch of red devils to trade that stuff you've got locked in that big chest.'

Joshua waited, all tensed up, but glaring defiantly at Floyd. Waiting for the big faker to pull out a pistol and blow him off the wagon. He wasn't too happy about that disturbing thought, but he had faced death in Abilene and he would look it in the eyes again rather than trade arms and whiskey to the Comanche, stirring them up to go out on killing and burning-out raids. To his surprise Floyd threw back his head and gave out a bellowing laugh.

'You're right about there being guns in that chest, Mr Webb,' Floyd said. 'There's a shotgun, and two rifles, and reloads for them and the guns I'm wearin'. But they ain't for tradin' with our red brethren. So you can bed down tonight without fearin'

I'll slit your throat.'

'Are you a hunter, Mr Goad?' Joshua asked. He waved an outstretched hand, taking in a broad sweep of the territory. 'If so, what the hell do you find to shoot out here? I ain't even seen a wild dog since we pulled out of Abilene.'

Floyd came to a quick decision. He opined that the kid wouldn't be staying long in the territory so it could do no harm for him to know the nature of his business. It would stop the kid from worrying thinking that he was sitting alongside some *comanchero* and in fear be crazy enough to pull a gun on him. It was still a fair haul to the camp and he didn't want the kid to quit on him.

'Bad asses, Mr Webb,' he said, his smile an all-toothed merciless grimace. 'I get paid by the Kansas/Pacific Railroad Company to hunt down bad-asses who raid their trains and rob the passengers. Right now, I'm after finding the men who dynamited the Forty-Mile cutting. That's where we're headin' for. I'm hopin' to pick up some sign that will

44

give me a lead to the perpetrators of the crime. If that don't rest easy with you, boy, you can quit here and now, and no offence will be taken.' He favoured Joshua with a fatherly smile. 'Though I'd appreciate it if you stayed till we get back to Abilene. That flea-bag, Ulysses, takes more note of you than me, who's watered and fed the ornery critter all these years.'

Joshua did some fast assaying of his own concerning his future, such as it was shaping up. Whatever way he took to get back to Abilene, the long trail on foot, or bumming a ride on a returning supply train flatcar, he'd still be broke. And it would be too dangerous for him to seek work in Abilene. The trail-hands who had tried to make him eat dirt might have left for Texas but other herds were coming up the trail, nursed by Texans who could have been told to shoot on sight a kid wearing a blue-belly sergeant's tunic.

He quickly came to the conclusion that his future didn't seem to stretch very far ahead.

If it did it would be as a raggedy-assed bum. If he opted to stay with Mr Goad he would get at least two squares a day and sleep more or less undercover. That he could probably stop a bullet meant for the big man if they caught up with the dynamiters they were tracking, were thoughts too far ahead for a kid who had been wondering where his next meal was coming from, to contemplate.

'I'd like to stay with the wagon till we get back to Abilene, Mr Goad,' he said. He gave a lopsided grin. 'There ain't anything pressing I oughta be doin'.'

Floyd smiled his gratitude. 'OK, Mr Webb, you're on the KP's payroll as from now.' Face hardening he added: 'But if things get rough you skat, *pronto*. I'm the *hombre* who's paid to take the shit, *comprende?*'

Josh grinned. '*Comprende*, boss,' he said, fork-tongued. One face-to-face pistol fight was all the excitement he craved in his life, yet he was willing to stand alongside Mr

Goad, come what may. He was beholden to the big man for more than just handling his ornery mule, he had saved his life, and while he hadn't done much with his life so far it was the only one he had and he wanted to live it out.

Floyd put out his hand. 'Shake, pard,' he said. 'Now move that mule's ass before more trouble hits the line.'

Six

Floyd broke camp at first light, being in some haste to check out what he honestly thought would be highly improbable leads on the dynamiters at the cutting, then back to Abilene to target his main, and only, suspect, Mr Turner Lazenby.

The wagon splashed its way across a shallow creek, and met trouble in the shape of three riders closing in on them from a stand of timber to the right of the trail, rifles held upright, butts on saddles, ready for instant action. They spread out across the trail, waiting for the wagon to come up to them. Joshua sensed Floyd stiffening up on the seat beside him.

'They may be ranch-hands stopping to pass the time of day with us,' Floyd said. 'Though the way they've spread themselves out I doubt it. If they bring those guns down on us, you pull that cannon of yours out fast and shoot that sonuvabitch out on the left. OK?'

Joshua had to swallow twice before a hoarse, 'OK' came out.

'Pull up here, Mr Webb,' Floyd said softly. 'Let them come to us.'

Joshua jerked Ulysses to a sudden halt and with sweat popping out of his ears, waited for the three riflemen to make their move, hoping that he would still be alive to discuss the meeting with Mr Goad when the gunsmoke settled. The sounds of creaking saddle-leather and stirrup irons as the riders walked their horses towards them rang like the bells of Hell in his ears. The wild hope that the men would turn out to be ranch-hands vanished as they pulled up close to the wagon. The gaunt, twitching-eyed faces that set his bowels churning again told him the worst.

'Howdy, gents,' Floyd said, genially, as though pleased to see company on the trail.

'Can I sell any of you some of my pills and medicines? Made from genuine Injun healin' herbs, and all guaranteed to cure what it says on the labels.'

It was a thin-faced, bearded rider who did the talking. 'Why don't you two pilgrims step down off that wagon, nice and easy-like, while me and the boys help ourselves to the pills, and whatever else that takes our fancy in your wagon.' Then he brought his rifle down to cover them, smiling as though he had cracked a joke.

A worried Joshua noticed that the road-agent's grin was as cheerless as Mr Goad's efforts. He also noted that the big man hadn't made his move and the evil-faced bastard had the drop on them. If he tried to go for his gun he would be dead for sure.

'Boy,' said Floyd, 'these *hombres* have us at a disadvantage. Do as he says, step down, we're not lookin' for trouble.' He got up slowly from the seat, arms outstretched from his sides, smiling his countryboy smile.

Joshua's heart sank. He couldn't believe

what he was witnessing. He looked up at Floyd in dismay. He had expected bolder action from the expert hunter of bad-asses, such as bold-eyeing the sons-of-bitches, and yanking out his Colts to deal out death, and he following suit, backing him up. Suddenly he heard the barking cough of a small pistol and Mr Goad's right hand seemed to sprout flame. The rider holding the rifle on them dropped his gun as he folded up in the middle like a burst feed sack and fell across his saddlehorn, dying fast before the fearful pain of the derringer ball tearing into his chest registered in his brain.

Then came the louder crack of a heavier calibre pistol that made Joshua flinch and the big man was fisting a smoking pistol in his left hand, and one of the other two men fell backwards off his horse. Then there was only one attacker left alive. Holy Moses! Joshua gasped, silently, the man he was supposed to put down! He made a frantic grab for his pistol when Floyd fired again, and the last saddle was emptied.

Sickly-faced apologetic, he looked up at Floyd. 'I wasn't much help was I, Mr Goad?' he said. 'It wasn't that I was scared. I've shot at men before. I was firing at reb marauders when I was only twelve when they came to burn us out. My pa's farm was on the Missouri/Kansas line. And Missourian free-staters weren't welcome neighbours in that neck of the woods. But everything happened so fast I kinda froze up.'

Floyd favoured him with a benign smile. 'That's the way it generally happens, boy,' he said. 'Killin' men, even assholes like those, is a chore you don't pick up as you go along, like ploughin' fields or shoeing horses. It comes kinda natural or you don't live long enough to become an expert.'

He didn't tell Joshua that if the would-be robbers had been real *pistoleros* instead of saddle-bums looking for easy pickings he and the kid would have been frozen for ever. He opined that the kid, once they reached the rail camp, would want to quit his service. Joshua felt like quitting right now. He would never make it as a gun-fighter. Only his pride and his earlier promise to himself to stay with Mr Goad prevented him from doing so. If a bare-assed savage Indian, he thought, set great store on his honour, losing face, he could do no less.

'I suppose we oughta give them a Christian burial, Mr Goad?' he said, eyeing, apprehensively, the last man shot, lying on his back, hat half over his face as though asleep, except that his right leg was twisted unnaturally beneath his body.

'We'll bury them to keep the varmints from feedin' off them, Mr Webb,' Floyd said. 'But they ain't havin' Christian prayers said over them. It won't do them any good, the sonsuvbitches are already stokin' up the fires of Hell.' He put his guns away and shrugged off his coat. 'OK, boy, let's raise some sweat and get those beauties planted.'

Seven

The trail dipped into a narrow, lush-grassed valley. Coming down the gentle slope, the wagon made its progress through forty or fifty grazing longhorns and, as they cornered the rock-faced edge of a spur ridge, Floyd and Joshua saw the house, a weathered, though sturdily built 'dobe and timber constructed building. Beyond it and several outbuildings they glimpsed the sparkling sheen of a creek.

'We can get rid of the horses here, Joshua,' Floyd said. The dead men's mounts were rope-tied to the tailgate of the wagon. 'Ulysses won't take kindly to sharing his grain with them; the temperamental critter could quit hauling the wagon. And we don't want to be asked awkward questions how we came by them. M'be we'll be allowed to

54

water Ulysses.'

Like the house, the three outbuildings were in good repair and the growing patch was well attended. The owner of the small ranch took a pride in his land. They could see no sign of the occupants of the house, though they soon made their presence felt, dramatically.

Something punched a hole in the side of the wagon with such force that the wagon swayed sideways on its springs, and ripped out planking as it exited through the other side. Then, from the cabin, they heard a dull boom and saw a wisp of grey smoke at one of the windows.

'Christ!' Joshua blurted out, gazing fearfully over his shoulder at the jagged-edged hole in the wagon's planking. 'What the hell is that? A field piece?'

'That's a Sharps .50 calibre rifle,' replied Floyd, narrow-eyeing the cabin. 'It can stop a buffalo dead in full stride at five hundred yards, and you can see what it can do to woodwork. Think of what it can do to us at this range. It's kiss-ass time for us, Mr Webb, pull up the wagon. Let's hope the *hombre* who has us in his sights is in the mood for talkin'.'

Floyd got to his feet, arms raised high above his head. 'Me and the boy are just passin' through,' he yelled. 'We thought this was open range. We're on our way to the spur-line camp. I'm hopin' to sell some of my medicines there! It's painted on the wagon who I am!'

The next few moments were some of the longest Floyd had ever experienced. He spent it silently cursing a blue streak. His investigation was turning out to be anything but a smooth running operation and could end right here. There had been the showdown with the Texans, the killing of the three saddle-tramps and now it seemed that he had landed in the middle of a range war of sorts. Why else was he being fired at on open range? One thing, he told himself morbidly, the end would come quick, either way. A man didn't get a nice clean winging wound from the lump of lead the big Sharps threw out. If it wasn't a fatal shot the loss of an arm or a badly smashed-up leg would see him on the way to Boot Hill in a pine box just as quickly, though more painfully.

He saw the cabin door swing open and a short, thickset man came out on to the porch with the long gun's barrel resting easy on his right shoulder, ready to swing down and send a death dealing ball winging on its way. Following him out was a young girl dressed in faded levis and checkered shirt. He also noticed that she was holding a rifle in front of her, handling it with the expertise of someone who knew more about long guns than which end the shell came out of. Men holding guns on him upset Floyd, females doing likewise, especially young, immature girls, scared the hell out of him.

Joshua was still naïve enough to have pleasanter thoughts towards the girl. Dark-haired, slim, round in the right places, even with men's clothes on, she seemed, at this distance, a good-looker. That such a beauty could shoot him dead didn't enter into his mind at all. Floyd saw his dreamy-eyed expression and cast him a jaundiced glare. The kid, he thought, would never make it as a lawman. He wouldn't have it in him to stop the kids in the street throwing stones at him.

'Your business better be what you state it is, mister!' Wade Carlson called out. 'Or you and the kid are in real trouble. You both stay up on the wagon, and you, kid, grab air like your big pard. I'm comin' across to have a looksee in that Noah's ark on wheels of yours. Any tricks and my daughter here, who's no mean shot, will cut you down.' Low voiced, Wade said, 'Cover the kid, Beth, and plug him if he goes for a gun.' He close-eyed her for a moment before adding, 'Can you do it, girl?'

'Yes, Pa,' Beth lied. She knew she could not bring herself to shoot the boy, about her own age, she thought, and wearing a Union tunic. She couldn't picture him as a no-good cattle-thief as her pa believed when they first saw the wagon driving down into the valley. Yet she had to back up her pa. Their lives, let alone their cattle could be lost if the big man and the boy were in cahoots with the three drifters they had scared off their range yesterday. If she had to fire she would try and wound the boy in the arm or leg, or deter him from making a move by putting a shell close by his head.

Then Beth had the wild crazy thought that if she wounded the boy she could maybe tend to his wounds, talk to him. Beth gave a slight winsome smile. Even talking to a boy, who could be a cattle thief, was better than talking to the critters on the ranch as she had been doing for the past three months till her pa was ready for the trip to Abilene for supplies for the winter. Then it wasn't so much as talking to the boys but fighting to keep their hands from pawing at her breasts and ass. She opined it wouldn't be a long conversation as her pa would want to string the boy up on one of the cottonwoods on the other side of the creek.

Floyd noted with some satisfaction that Joshua hadn't frozen up again but had raised his hands. Any hesitation on his part not to have done so would have been read as a hostile act and the kid would have found out that being shot by a pretty girl was every bit as painful as being shot by her pa.

Floyd smiled real good as the rancher came up closer. By the cut of the hard, weather-tanned face, he didn't seem a man who could be fooled by a pill-pedlar's oily salesman smile. He did have the temptation to flick out the derringer, but a quick glance at the girl on the porch saw that she looked very business-like with the rifle up to her shoulder, all set to pull off a load. And he was paying the kid to drive the wagon not to get lumps shot off him. The time wasn't yet ripe for the showing of the derringer.

'I'm Doctor Floyd T. Goad,' Floyd said, gazing on the black hexagonal hole of the Sharps' muzzle, his smile making his jaws ache. He jerked his head sideways. 'You can see it painted up on the wagon.' His grin stretched out another inch. 'Leastways you could'uv if you hadn't blown it away with your piece.'

Wade Carlson shot him a dark suspicious look. 'M'be you are this Doc fella,' he said. 'Then m'be you ain't. What I want to know is where's the *hombre* who owns that piebald you've got tied to the back of your wagon? Yesterday I cleared him and his two buddies off my land with this.' Wade tapped the barrel of the Sharps. 'The sonsuvbitches were after liftin' some of my beef. They ain't in the back of the wagon hopin' to sneak up on me?'

'Friend,' said Floyd, 'me and my pard had a run in with those three boys earlier on in the day. Right now they'll be doing their cattle-liftin' in Hell.'

Wade favoured Floyd with a disbelieving look then he noticed that the big man's smile though still cracking the heavy-jowled face, was as cheerful as a Comanche buck's killing grin. Wade sensed rather than saw a blur of movement from the pill doctor and found he was gazing into the twin muzzles of a small handgun, which he knew, with a cold feeling in his belly, could kill as effectively at this range as the Sharps. He cursed. It was too late to bring up the Sharps, the big bastard had the drop on him. He no longer doubted that the 'doc' and his *compadre* had out-shot the three saddle-bums.

'Now why don't we end this Mexican standoff, mister?' Floyd said. 'I'm sure you don't want that purty girl over there to witness a bloody shootout, and me and the boy here have had our fill of killin' for the day.'

Wade glimpsed the same slick hand movement and the fisted hideaway gun disappeared, and the big man's smile was friendly again. It was quick-decision time and Wade made one. He lowered the barrel of the Sharps to the ground, then turned and yelled, 'It's OK, Beth! Tell Ma she can put her gun down and get some coffee goin'!' He looked back at Floyd, grinning.

'You ain't the only *hombre* with a hidden back-up gun, friend. Ma was raised in Kaintuck, Blue Ridge country. And even the kids there could shoot straight before they could walk straight.'

'If me and my pard weren't peaceful men,' Floyd said, mock serious, 'we could have had us a real war goin' on here.'

'We live in wild times, Doc,' replied Wade. 'And a man has to do what he must to protect his family and property. Bring your wagon in: there's a creek behind the house where you can water your horses. I'm Wade Carlson, the girl with the rifle is my daughter Beth.' He grinned. 'I take it you ain't a real doctor of medicine, Doc.'

'I never did get down to workin' my way through medical school,' Floyd said, smiling broadly. 'But my name is as it says so on the wagon. My pard is called Joshua Webb who hails from Missouri. And as I said we're travellin' to the rail camp to try and earn ourselves a living.'

Beth had taken Joshua and the animals to the creek, leaving Floyd and Wade sitting on the porch, the rancher drawing on his pipe, Floyd chewing at the end of a foul-smelling cheroot. Mrs Carlson came out on to the porch with coffee and freshly baked cookies. In spite of her age and the back-breaking work and worry she must have put in helping her husband run the ranch and bring up her daughter, her face still held the traces of beauty with which her daughter was blessed. She had given him a firm handshake and eyed him with a no-nonsense look that made him think that Mrs Carlson, if put to the test, would have blown him and Joshua off the wagon seat as ably as she could obviously cook.

Wade, equally searching-eyed, assessed his guest. He was getting the feeling that in spite of a wagonload of pills and patent medicines, the big man's reasons for being in the territory went a lot deeper than selling his quack cures. While he realized that suchlike characters ran the risk of being run out of town and needed to be armed to protect themselves, the sleeve gun, the holster bulge under his left arm, and the pistol sticking out of his pants top, seemed a lot of hardware for a quack-doctor to be toting around. Wade, being a plainsman, didn't think it right for him to poke his nose in a stranger's business, so he kept his thoughts to himself.

Floyd, guessing what was passing through the rancher's mind decided to enlighten him. He had to start asking questions sometime and Wade, he judged, was a man who would keep a buttoned-up lip. He grinned. 'I reckon by the way you've been eyein' my guns you're having doubts about me bein' a pill-pedlar, Wade. Well, you're right. I ain't. I'm a Kansas Pacific railroad agent. I'm here to seek out the murderin' sonsuvbitches who blew up the line cutting.'

Wade raised a quizzical eyebrow. 'The kid seems a mite young to be a hard-nosed regulator.'

Floyd laughed. 'He ain't. I just kinda

picked him up in Abilene.' He then told Wade about the trouble with the Texans. 'I'm bankin' on the Texans being on their way home by the time I've finished scoutin' around the cuttin' lookin' for sign and make it back to town. Then the kid can go his own way. And I don't have to worry about him gettin' shot in a business that he ain't part of.' Floyd grinned. 'Though I got the feelin' that the young blood wouldn't have minded too much being winged by your daughter.'

'The boy can stay here, Floyd,' Wade said. 'My only hand lit out to join up with a Texas outfit for more pay.'

Floyd broke off the conversation as he saw Joshua and Beth leading the animals back from the creek. Joshua's broad grin seemed to have been pasted on his face. Even the normally sour-faced Ulysses had a bright-eyed look about him. Floyd sighed silently, but feelingly. It had been a long, long time since a pretty, innocent girl had smiled sweetly at him.

'Grab the kid now, Wade,' he said. 'He'll

work his guts out for you for two squares a day and a blanket in the barn. Your daughter's got him mesmerized. I'll check out the cuttin' on my own.'

'No, you take the boy, Floyd,' Wade insisted. 'Four eyes are better lookin' for sign than two. If he wants the job you can drop him off when passin' this way on the trip back to Abilene.' Then changing the subject, Wade asked Floyd if he had any likely suspects lined up as the possible dynamiters.

Floyd had already told the rancher who he was; he might as well take him fully into his confidence, so he told him of his suspicions. 'Well, kinda, Wade. Mr Turner Lazenby, the freight owner. Though it's only an old lawman's gut-feeling, I ain't got anything against him I could put up in front of a judge.' He expected the same reaction from Wade regarding Lazenby's possible involvement with the dynamiters as he'd had from Silas Black. To his surprise Wade agreed with his choice of a suspect.

'Yeah, I can see your reasonin'','Wade said. 'Lazenby will lose more than most in Abilene if the spur line goes through. Though there'll be a lot more than Lazenby's takin' a financial nosedive when the line's operational, the stage line, the saloon owners when there's no Texans bellying-up to their bars. But givin' it some thought, Lazenby would be my strongest guess as the man behind the trouble on the line. He has some hard men on his payroll who wouldn't lose any sleep over blowin' up a cuttin' if the pay suited them.'

'All I've got to do, Wade,' Floyd said, 'is to find some proof against Lazenby that will stand up in a court of law. And that isn't going to be easy with him being a leading citizen and all.'

'I don't know if it's significant or not,' Wade said, 'but the day the cuttin' was blown up three of Lazenby's men passed by here headin' for Abilene, ridin' hell-for-leather. Of course, they could have been ridin' back from escorting a wagon-train to

Newton but I've no recollection of seeing any of Lazenby's wagons pass by for over two weeks.'

'Could be another pointer towards Lazenby's guilt,' replied Floyd, thoughtfully. 'I'll see if I can pick up any tracks of three men at the cuttin' and follow them through.'

'You take care doing it, Floyd,' Wade warned. 'Mort Behen was one of the three riders. He's Lazenby's straw boss, an ex-reb Missouri guerilla. He's got a rep as a bushwhackin' killer. As merciless as any who carried out dirty business in that part of the territory. Mort is a mean-faced bastard, sits up of a fancy silver-worked Mex saddle. If you come up against him don't hesitate one second to plug him.'

'If Mr Behen's one of the men behind the killin' at the cuttin',' Floyd said, soberly, 'I'll put him down for keeps with the greatest of pleasure.' He got on to his feet. 'Now, I think it's time I thanked your good lady for the coffee and chow and got on the trail to the rail camp. And I'd be obliged if you could take the three horses off my hands.' He smiled. 'I'll give the kid another ten minutes of happiness. Though when you tell him you want to hire him that wagon of mine will burn up the trail to the rail camp.'

While they were watering the animals at the creek, Beth was having her wish fulfilled, talking to a boy, and one, thank the Lord, she hadn't had to shoot. She asked Joshua all about himself, knowing that in half an hour or so he would be going out of her life for ever. Unless, she thought, she could somehow persuade him to stay.

Joshua, all smiles at the unexpected pleasure of being in the company of a pretty girl who was really showing an interest in him, needed no prodding to answer her questions. He was also aware that the good time wouldn't last long.

'Did you and Mr Goad kill those three men, Mr Webb?' Beth asked. 'I heard Mr Goad tell Pa that the men tried to rob you....'

Though Joshua wanted to give Beth the

impression that he was one tough *hombre* who could handle himself well in a shoot-out, he didn't want to be shown up as a lying, scared-stiff kid in case she heard later through her pa that Mr Goad had to do all the killing. He just gave a tough *hombre*'s non-committal grin. 'I only backed up Mr Goad,' he said, and left Beth to work out her own interpretation of the gunfight.

The horses and Ulysses had been watered and Joshua knew, albeit reluctantly, that it was time for the sweet-talking to come to an end.

'It's time I was hitchin' Ulysses on to the wagon, Miss Beth,' he said, grinning wryly. 'Mr Goad will be wanting to move on to the rail camp. I think we're givin' the horses to your pa.'

Beth realized that if she wanted Joshua to stay it was time she said her piece. Plunging in, she said, 'Pa's lookin' for a ranch hand, Mr Webb. I know you're working for the railroad so I don't suppose you'd want....' Her voice trail away as she gazed doe-eyed at him. She knew she was expecting a lot from a man she had only known for such a short time, and who already had a well-paid job with the railroad company, to work for what wages her pa could afford.

Joshua's heart missed several beats. He had just been offered the chance of a future, and a pleasant one at that, if he hadn't already made a promise to himself to stay with Mr Goad till his investigation was over. Keeping his disappointment from showing in his face and voice he said, 'I ain't actually workin' for the Kansas Pacific, Miss Beth, it's Mr Goad who hired me. He's here to track down the men who blew up the cuttin' and it's kinda beholden on me to stay till it's all cleared up. But once the men have been brought to justice, if your pa still wants me, I'll gladly work for him, and that's a promise.' The words had come rushing out, not giving him time to think that when the showdown came with the dynamiters he might end up dead.

Beth, raised in a land which had seen

more than its fair share of violence and bloodshed, by white and red men, was thinking the same disturbing thoughts. Her sweet-smiling masked her deep concern. 'You come back here when Mr Goad no longer needs you, Mr Webb,' she said. 'I'll tell Pa he needn't look for anyone else, I'll work twice as hard till then.'

With a broad grin that would have matched Floyd's in its width and falseness, Joshua hid his own miserable thoughts. 'You do that, Miss Beth,' he said. 'I'll be back. Now let's get Ulysses ready for moving out.'

All the Carlsons stood on the porch and watched their visitors move out. Floyd saw that Joshua and Beth were looking down in the mouth. He couldn't understand why. After all, in a couple of days or so, he would be back at the ranch, permanently. Kids, he caustically concluded, were all soft inside nowadays.

Pulling out of the valley with Joshua still sitting glum-faced and not speaking, Floyd reckoned it was time his mule-skinner snapped out of his black mood. 'I'd thought you'd be doin' handsprings all the way to the line camp, kid,' he said. 'Gettin' yourself hired by Mr Carlson and bein' able to see more of the purty Miss Beth.'

Without taking his eyes off the trail ahead, Joshua said, 'I turned down the job, Mr Goad. I told Beth she would have to wait till we caught the men who blew up the cuttin', bein' that I was beholden to you till then.'

Floyd looked at him in amazement. 'Turned the job down! Beholden to me! I told Wade I'd drop you off at the ranch after we'd finished our scouting for tracks at the cuttin'.' He fierce-eyed Joshua. 'And that's what I intend doin'. What crazy debt do you figure you owe me? The run-in with those Texas drovers? It was my choice to partake in that business. If you think that you owe me you've paid it off by keepin' hold of that big-eared sonuvabitch pullin' this wagon, and the trackin' you're goin' to do for me at the camp.'

Floyd's face and voice softened. 'Mr

Webb,' he said, 'what trouble may happen on the line is the business of the railroad: that means yours truly. You've got your own life to live and you've got the chance to make it a fair one. Take it. Killin' men and riskin' your own neck ain't a sociable way of livin' at all, believe me.' Floyd grabbed the reins from Joshua and pulled Ulysses to a neck-jerking stop. 'Now, Mr Webb,' he said, 'you unhitch your *compadre,* Ulysses there, and ride barebacked like an Injun buck to tell that purty girl you have strong feelin's for her, that her pa has got himself a new hand. It ain't heart-warmin' travelling with a sour-tempered mule: sitting alongside a like-minded kid ain't goin' to make it any happier for me.'

A wide-grinning Joshua leapt off the wagon, whooping like the Indian he supposed to be. In no time at all he was raising the dust along their back trail to the Carlsons.

Floyd leaned back against the side of the wagon, relaxing on the seat. His lips curled in a slight smile of satisfaction. For the first time in his career as a hunter of bad-asses he had given someone a bright future; normally the only future he offered men was the choice of a grave or a prison cell. He hoped he wasn't getting religion. He would still have to be one mean son-of-a-bitch to face the backshooter, Mr Mort Behen.

Eight

Three hours travelling south of Wade Carlson's ranch, Floyd noticed that the trail swung westwards, closing in on the new line. At the same time, two riders came out of a hollow at the side of the trail and rode up to the wagon. Hard-faced, watchful-eyed men, double-armed men. Floyd opined that they were some of the extra guards Silas Black had said he had posted along the line.

'Expectin' trouble, friends?' Floyd said, greeting them with a big smile.

'The Kansas Pacific Railroad Company is, friend,' one of the riders said. 'That's why I'm gonna take a peek in the back of your wagon.'

'Whatever you're seekin' you won't find in there,' Floyd said. 'I'm only carryin' what's stated on the wagon's sides, pills and medicines. I'm Doctor Floyd T. Goad, this is my assistant, Mr Webb. We're headin' for the line camp, hopin' to sell some of our cures to the boys there.'

The rider who was doing the talking spat a stream of tobacco juice between his horse's ears. 'I wouldn't give any of your *cures* to a sick dog, and I hate dogs. Chuck, just point your Winchester at the fat man there. If he so much as farts, shoot him. I'll take a look inside the wagon.' He kneed his horse to the rear of the wagon and pushing aside the tarp cover, eased himself out of his saddle and over the tailgate and into the wagon.

Floyd heard the rattle of jars and bottles as, not too gently, the guard rummaged around the wagon's contents. 'What's in the chest, fat man?' he heard the guard call out.

Still keeping a wary eye on Chuck, Floyd shouted over his shoulder. 'Some extra guns and boxes of reloads, that's all. Self-protection. Every *hombre* you meet up with along the trail ain't as sociable as you two gents.'

Floyd and Joshua involuntarily lifted ass several inches from the seat at the sudden, deafening explosion of a gunshot in the confined space of the wagon. Even the steel-nerved Ulysses was startled enough to kick out his back legs in alarm and cut loose with a yellow-toothed snarling bray.

'I've a key for that padlock, mister,' Floyd grated angrily. 'You only had to ask.' He turned his head and looked at Joshua. 'That's the trouble with this world, Mr Webb, people's manners ain't what they used to be, and that's a fact.'

They heard the guard climb back out of the wagon and say, 'They're clean, Chuck. They're not shippin' in any dynamite.'

Chuck pushed his rifle back into its boot. 'OK, pill man,' he said, 'you can get your wagon rollin' again. Though I think that you're givin' that mule of yours a heap of sweat for nothin'. You ain't gonna sell any of your quack cures to the Mick gangers. If you was haulin' whiskey and lewd wimmin' I'd reckon you'd earn yourselves a dollar or two. I hope there's no hard feelin's: we're only doin' what we've been paid to do.'

Though he had to restrain himself from bending a Colt barrel over the head of the man who had blown open his chest, Floyd tried to look as though he hadn't been too upset at having a Winchester aimed, and ready to cut loose at him. He replied, 'No hard feelin's, friend, but I reckon the railroad company owes me another oak chest.'

Chuck laughed. 'Did you hear that, Billy?' He hard-eyed Floyd. 'Listen, you fake croaker, think yourself lucky we spotted your wagon before it got any nearer to the line or you'd be suing the KP for a new head. The company's been havin' a heap of trouble lately and we've got orders to shoot on sight any *hombre* prowlin' around the new track.'

Floyd let out a long, low whistle. He was prepared to risk getting himself shot in the service of the railroad, he never expected to get shot by employees of the KP. But he had to remember that he was fighting in a kind of war and he wouldn't be the first man to be shot by his own side. It was another dimension of risk he had to face as a regulator. Floyd, he told himself, if you don't quit this business soon you ain't going to grow much older in one piece.

'OK, Mr Webb,' he said. 'Let's bid these two gents goodbye and get this wagon rolling on to the end-of-the-line camp or Ulysses will have to haul this wagon all the way to Newton.'

Turner Lazenby was sitting at the poker table with Poker Alice, Silas Black, and Jeb Blunt, the town marshal, his mind not on the cards he held in his hand.

Mort Behen's report that he and his men hadn't picked out any possible undercover railroad investigators or Pinkerton agents, stepping off trains or stage coaches pulling into their depots since the dynamiting, had reduced him to nail-biting nervousness. There had been plenty of hard-eyed, city-suited men arriving in town, but they had been checked out as hard-hearted cattle buyers. And no strangers were making the rounds of the saloons and bars asking questions about the raid.

It seemed that the KP was making no effort to find out who was trying to wreck their line. Seemingly, thought Lazenby morosely. The reality, he could feel it in his bones, was that the KP agent, or agents, had sneaked into Abilene unnoticed by Behen and his men, and were already at work snooping around, ready to finger people. He shivered.

Keeping the desperation out of his voice he said, 'Any progress on finding out the men who are damaging the spur line, Jeb?' He had wanted to ask Silas Black directly about the KP's own investigations but dared not: he didn't want to show an undue interest in the railroad's troubles. He hoped the marshal would give him the answers he wanted to settle his nerves. Lazenby was to be disappointed.

'Naw,' Marshal Blunt replied. 'Me and my deputies rode out to the cuttin' and took a good scout around. They could have been Injuns who did the dynamitin' for all the sign we cut. We couldn't get even a smell of the murderin' sonsuvbitches, beggin' your pardon, Poker Alice. My boys are keepin' their ears open when they do their nightly patrols of the saloons for any loose-mouth talk that might give us a lead. But, as I told Silas here, I've got my hands full keepin' a lid on the town when the Texicans are bayin' at the moon. How are your agents doin', Silas?'

Silas Black was all set to blurt out that he expected some results soon, as the KP's top regulator had already started his investigations but Lazenby's tight-assed look made him hold back the information. Something, Silas thought, was gnawing away at the freight-owner's innards. A great deal more worrying than his current run of bad luck at cards. Suddenly, he thought, Floyd's hinting that Lazenby could be the man behind the raids didn't seem all that way out.

And secrecy being Floyd's guiding word, he said, 'I don't know what's happening, Marshal. I'm in the dark as much as you are. I suppose any agents they send down will contact me. I've had a wire from head office that they've got things in hand. If they do contact me you'll be the first to know.' His suspicions against Lazenby deepened as he noticed his face seemed more pinched looking. Somehow he managed to control his temper and held back from throwing his cards into Lazenby's face and accusing him openly as a murderous son-of-a-bitch. He forced a grin. 'Now let's get on with the game, folks,' he said. 'I feel my luck's in tonight. Raise me, Poker Alice, or fold.'

Behen, thinking along the same lines as Lazenby, that the KP's agents were already in the territory, if not actually in Abilene, instead of fretting that he had failed to spot them, was about to take measures to flush them out. The Missouri brush-boys during the war weren't noted for sitting on their asses and waiting for an unseen enemy to close in on them. Quantrill and 'Bloody' Bill Anderson were masters of the keep-hitting-'em school of warfare. So Behen knew from experience that attack was the best form of defence.

The attack he contemplated making was against a six-span wooden trestle bridge across which the track ran, clearing a deep, dry wash. When the bridge blew sky-high Behen opined that every undercover KP agent would be scurrying around the territory like a nest of disturbed ants. Behen grim-smiled. Once they had shown themselves it would give him great pleasure to put them down for keeps.

He knew that the bridge would be guarded by at least two men. Once it was dark, Pablo, part-Indian, part-several-other-blood-lines, an expert with a knife, should clear an unopposed way to the bridge for them without raising a general alarm.

'Pike,' he said, 'get hold of Al before he

downs too much redeye. We've got work to do. Me and Pablo will meet you at the usual place.'

An hour later, riding singly out of town, the four riders met up at the rendezvous, a derelict stage way station two miles out on the Newton trail, Behen opining that four men were sufficient to do the job, and had less chance of being spotted moving on to the bridge than a bigger bunch of riders. Assured by Pablo that no one was trailing them, Behen gave a grin.

'OK, boys,' he said. 'Let's go and blow us up a Union bridge and make "Bloody" Bill Anderson smile in Hell.'

Nine

Phil Spenser scowled as he saw the wagon cut off from the main trail and head towards the rail-camp. He could make out its garish colours and guessed that its owner was some oily-tongued drummer of sorts wanting to earn himself a few fast bucks. What the drummer would be offering for sale, Spenser opined, would be rotgut moonshine labelled as genuine Irish whiskey. The drummer would be told to turn his wagon round and seek new pastures, even if he had to do the asking holding a gun on him. Spenser had seen Irish gangers drunk, they acted wilder than drunken Comanche.

A slow smile crept into his face, the first since the dynamiting at the cutting, as he recognized the big, burly man sitting next to the young kid doing the driving.

'Well, I'll be damned!' he breathed. 'Mr Floyd T. Goad!' The Kansas Pacific had sure pulled out all the stops to catch the men who were delaying the building of the spur line, he thought. He suppressed a laugh as he read the slogans on the wagon side, the railroad's chief trouble-shooter posing as a quack doctor. And, he had to admit, the fat son-of-a-bitch looked the part; it was up to him to keep the pretence going.

As the wagon drew up alongside him he said angrily, loud enough for the nearest of the railroad crew to hear, 'This is a dry camp, friend. If you're a whiskey-pedlar fronting as a pill merchant then you've wasted your time making the trip here.' Then he gave Floyd a wink.

Floyd replied with a slight acknowledging tilt of his head before saying, in a loud, blustering, self-righteous tone, 'I don't deal in the demon drink, sir! Nor do I have dealin's with lewd women, in case you're thinkin' that I've some suchlike females in the back of my wagon! I'm Doctor Floyd T. Goad, endeavourin' to sell some of my genuine Indian potions to your men. They will keep them free from many ailments, so you'll get more work out of them.'

'Indian medicines, my ass.' Spenser barked, enjoying his verbal sparring with Floyd. 'The worthless rubbish you're pedling hasn't been anywhere near an Indian. You and the kid there will have made up the concoctions in the back of your wagon.' Spenser gave Floyd a significant glance, nodding towards Joshua as he did so. Getting an OK nod from Floyd he began speaking again. 'Any luck, Floyd?' he asked, in a much lower voice.

'Just a suspicion, that's all, Phil,' replied Floyd. 'But the sighting of three riders ass-kickin' it from this direction back to Abilene by a rancher, on the day of the dynamitin' kinda strengthens that suspicion.'

'Three riders, eh,' Spenser repeated reflectively. 'We looked for signs of the sonsuvbitches at the cutting but we came up with a big fat zero. We couldn't tell if there had been three, or thirty-three riders there.'

'That figures,' said Floyd. 'No offence, Phil, but your boys have been scoutin' for sign in the wrong place. One of the riders I mentioned is an ex-Missouri guerilla. Those *hombres* were damn clever in coverin' their back trails. My feelin' is that the dynamiters came in on foot, feet makin' less sign than horses' hooves.' Floyd gave the land a long, thoughtful look before saying, 'They'd leave their horses on that rocky ridge back there,' he said. 'Come down it to get on the main trail again when they'd done their work. But as you see, the hard ground peters out before it meets the Newton trail.' Floyd grinned. 'If I'm thinkin' right, and it ain't been rainin' since the dynamitin', there m'be should be the tracks of three riders at that spot. If there ain't I'll have to get me another suspect.'

'If you're intending to go out looking for sign, Floyd,' Phil said. 'You watch out for my men. They're–'

'We've already met up with two of them,' interrupted Floyd. 'They seemed a mite disappointed that we didn't give them an excuse to put holes in us.'

'They take their work seriously,' Phil replied. 'They've got a lot of track to cover and determined men, especially at night, could still break through and damage the line. We're relying on you to rope them in and expose the man at the back of this skulduggery, pronto-like.'

Floyd gave a non-committal grunt. 'I'll do what I can, Phil, but I'm starting off blind. Now if you ride out with us it'll look to any unfriendly eyes, as though you're runnin' us outa camp. And it'll stop your boys from jumpin' us again.'

Floyd was driving the wagon, Joshua, having the keenest eyes according to Floyd, was walking slightly away from the trail looking intensely for the tracks of three horses to prove Floyd's reasoning right. Then they could head back to Abilene, leaving him at the Carlson ranch with Beth.

He moved several more yards from trail as they came up to the ridge and almost immediately struck paydirt. He raised his hand and yelled. 'There's tracks here, Mr Goad!'

Floyd stepped down from the wagon, watching carefully where he placed his feet. He walked over to Joshua and looked down at where he was pointing. Spenser drew up his horse and kept it stationary on the trail, not wanting to mess up any possible tracks of the dynamiters.

'They're in line with the ridge, Mr Goad,' Joshua said, eagerly. 'And there's definitely tracks of three horses!'

'The sonsuvbitches got careless in their hurry to get clear of the territory after the big bang,' Floyd said. 'If they had hit the trail ahead of us they would have kept on hard ground and left no signs of their presence at all. Good work, Mr Webb. Mort Behen and two of his boys made those tracks, Phil, so you can guess who I'm figurin' is the man who's payin' them to raid the line.'

'Lazenby,' gasped Phil. 'I would never have believed it.'

'Neither did Silas Black, Phil,' Floyd said. 'But it takes all sorts to make a world. We've done all we can here so we'll head back to Abilene and see what I can dig up there.'

Spenser wished them both good luck and good hunting then stayed to watch the wagon rolling south along the trail to Newton for a while, thinking with grim satisfaction that Lazenby, Behen, or whoever else was responsible for sabotaging the line, their days were numbered. Floyd T. Goad, once he smelt his prey, didn't hesitate in going in for the kill. Then he turned his horse round and rode back to the camp.

Well south of the line camp Floyd gave Joshua the order to cut off from the trail and head eastwards for a spell so that when they finally turned north, back to Abilene, they would pass clear of the camp. A wide-grinning Joshua yanked hard on the left-hand rein and yelled. 'Move ass, Ulysses! A purty girl's waitin' for me!'

Ten

Darkness was dropping in on the trail and Joshua could see the gleam of a campfire away to his left, in the direction of the spur line.

'I reckon that's the camp of the two guards who checked us out, Mr Goad,' he said, nodding in the direction of the fire.

The big man clicked his tongue, disapprovingly, not speaking, as though in deep thought. Joshua guessing that Floyd wasn't in the mood for small talk did some thinking of his own: of how his luck had suddenly changed for the better; how his future relationship with the pretty Miss Beth could develop. The curt order of, 'Pull off the trail, Mr Webb,' broke into his pleasant thoughts.

'There's still enough light for us to make a

few more miles, Mr Goad,' Joshua said, eager to reach the Carlson ranch as soon as he could when they broke camp at daybreak.

'We make camp here,' Floyd said, firm-voiced. 'And it will be a cold camp.' Joshua saw the flash of Floyd's teeth as he gave him one of this wide but cheerless smiles. 'No fires.'

'No fires?' repeated Joshua.

'You heard right, boy,' replied Floyd. 'This ain't some picnic ride we're on. We're tryin' to track down a bunch of murderous assholes. Who's to say that they're not hunkered down somewhere out here. They ain't quit hittin' the railroad yet so we can't take any chances that there's only us and the night critters on the move around here. We'll bed down in that stand of cotton-woods to the right of us.'

Joshua, not for the first time, realized that he had a lot to learn about the man-hunting business. He tugged at the right rein, bringing Ulysses round in the direction of the trees.

'Now those two fellas whose campfire we just passed,' Floyd said, 'ain't doing any guardin' at all. They're not even looking out for themselves by letting anyone who comes by this way, on legal or illegal business, know where they are. Cold and alive, Mr Webb, is a damn sight better than endin' up cold and dead. You'd agree with that statement, Mr Webb, wouldn't you?'

Joshua gave a grunted, begrudged yes, his thoughts still lingering on the disappointing fact that it would be later than he hoped before he saw Miss Beth again. He guided the wagon between the trees till he saw that it would be shielded from sight of any rider coming along the trail.

Joshua had seen to the unhitching of Ulysses, fed and watered him and was now sitting alongside Floyd spooning cold beans down him. Long ways different from the meal Mrs Carlson had laid before them, he thought nostalgically.

'You take the first watch, Mr Webb,' Floyd said. 'I'll try and get a little shuteye in the back of the wagon.' He handed Joshua a big-faced, gun-metal timepiece. 'Give me two hours unless you hear anything suspicious, *comprende*? If it turns out to be a false alarm I don't mind. As I said, our lives are at stake and we'd be foolish to take chances.'

The moon had clouded over and the darkness under the trees was almost absolute. Josh passed his watch thinking of how things would be when he was working for Mr Carlson, smiling to himself like some village idiot. There was no danger of him falling asleep on guard if his mind had been a blank, the trip-hammer-like tick of Floyd's watch would have woken up a corpse. It was Ulysses who gave the alarm. He heard the mule give a low snorting neigh and thought that a snake or night bird had brushed close by the animal, scaring or annoying it.

Then he heard a slight noise behind him and Floyd was standing at his side, face hard and alert, peering into the darkness, back along the trail.

'Mr Webb,' he said, still gazing into the

night. 'Arm yourself.'

Joshua reckoned that his eyesight was as good if not better than the older Mr Goad yet he could not see anything to be alarmed at. Curious, he said, 'What have you seen, Mr Goad?'

To his surprise the answer was, 'Not a damn thing, Mr Webb.' Floyd grinned. 'I ain't blessed with second sight, kid, but Ulysses is the most cantankerous mule this side of the Mississippi, horses being his pet hate. He's just let us know he can smell horses out there somewhere. They could be ranch hands riding back to their spreads, men from the rail-camp, or the fellas we're after. It won't hurt us none to think the worst. It's a perfect night for them to do their villainous work. We'll go and have a look to see if my reasonin' is right. One thing, Mr Webb, don't fire till I do if we run into trouble, then cut loose fast. And stick close by me; it's hair-trigger time and purty Miss Beth would never forgive me if I accidentally plugged you.'

Joshua gave Floyd a sickly grin. Shoot-outs, he decided were becoming more dangerous. He picked up a Winchester and jumped off the wagon. Floyd joined him and they both made their way through the trees to the trail.

Eleven

Chuck got up from the fire, breaking wind as he stretched himself. 'I'll do the first night watch at the bridge, Billy,' he said. 'Keep the coffee hot for when I get back.' He rolled a makings and lit it up before walking across to his horse.

Pablo ceased his belly-crawling towards the fire and dropped flat on seeing one of the guards get to his feet. Coming in on the camp he had picked out two men at the fire, then, swinging wide of it, had moved silently down to the bridge. There he had waited for several minutes, listening, watching in the darkness in the wash till he was satisfied that he had only two men to deal with. Though the silent killing of two men at the camp, where the light from their fire would prevent him from getting in real close, was a tricky business, he fancied himself as a real expert with a knife.

He had to kill the guards. Behen and the boys, bedded down 200 yards behind him were waiting impatiently for his all-clear signal. They would be eager to get their hands on the money they would be paid for destroying the bridge.

He saw the guard mount his horse. Pablo grinned. The boys were going to get their spending money after all. He got to his feet and in a crouching run, got ahead of the rider.

Chuck nosed his horse down into the wash, lowering his head to clear the cross timbers of the first span. Pablo dropped down on to his horse like some gigantic, blood-sucking bat. Before Chuck could warn off his attacker, or shout a warning to Billy, an arm was round his neck, snapping his head back, choking off his cry of alarm. Then he felt the coldness of steel on his skin, and, in the last few minutes of his life, the warmness of his blood streaming down his neck from the fearsome gash at his throat.

Pablo held the guard till his body ceased its struggling and slumped back against him. Hands sticky with blood, he pulled the dead man's feet from the stirrups and pushed him out of the saddle. He calmed down the horse, skitterish at the smell of blood, and rode out of the creek, the killing knife and his hands wiped clean on the horse's flanks.

'Everything OK?' Billy called out. 'You ain't been long.'

A knife blade glinting in flight from the light of the fire gave Billy the too-late warning that it wasn't Chuck up on Chuck's horse. He fell backwards to the ground with the knife buried hilt deep in his chest, his hand still clutching the half-drawn pistol, dying a less messy death than Chuck had, but just as quickly.

Pablo leapt from the horse, pulled the knife out of his victim's body, wiping it on the dead guard's shirt and slipped it back into its fancy-worked sheath. He then cupped his hands to his mouth and gave the all-clear call to Behen and the boys.

Floyd heard the hoot of an owl and froze in his tracks, putting out a hand to draw Joshua to a halt beside him. 'That owl don't fly, Mr Webb,' he growled softly. 'I figure that we're too late to be of any help to the guards. There, see!'

Joshua picked out the blurred silhouettes of several riders moving across their front. 'Ulysses ain't such a dumb critter as he looks, Mr Goad,' he said.

'That he ain't, Mr Webb, that he ain't,' Floyd replied, soberly. 'Though sometimes I wish he had the brains to use a rifle. There's too many of the sonsuvbitches for you and me to tangle with in a head-on shoot-out. But m'be we can scare them off from what mischief they're bent on at the track.'

Josh gave the body lying beside the fire a nervous, apprehensive glance. He had heard from Floyd the mayhem the gang they were trailing were capable of, now he could see some of it for himself. He gripped his rifle tighter till his knuckles cracked and swore that he wouldn't let Floyd down this time by freezing up.

'They must be at the bridge,' he heard Floyd say, as a dark, high shape set against the backdrop of a starlit sky came into his view. They advanced several more yards before Floyd called a halt and gave him his final orders.

'Move a few yards to your right,' Floyd said. 'But don't go pushing forward.' Floyd gave Joshua a snarl of a smile. 'That means, Mr Webb, any *hombre* in front of us is fair game, because I sadly fear the other guard has paid the price for his carelessness. And don't keep firing from the same spot, shift around somewhat then they can't pinpoint you and it'll keep them guessin' just how many of us there are. We start the shindig by cuttin' loose with half a magazine from the Winchesters, nonstop, sweeping under the bridge. That oughta rattle the sonsuvbitches. Then we pick 'em off when and where we see them. OK?'

Joshua only nodded his OK: his throat was too dry with fear and an excitement to voice it.

Behen and Pike had stayed up on their horses on each side of the wash, acting as lookouts. Al, standing on his saddle, was helping Pablo, crouched like a monkey on the struts of the bridge, to back the sticks of dynamite under the central span. Behen was well pleased with the smoothness of the operation, another few minutes and the line would be out of use for several months, maybe for good, he hoped. Which would bring him and his boys a good bonus from Lazenby.

He heard Pablo call a low, 'OK', to Al, and guessed he was ready for the fuse wire to be laid along the bed of the wash, long enough for them to be out of range of the shattered timbers that would come showering down when the plunger was pressed. The sudden echoing rattling of a fusillade of shots ended, dramatically, Behen's optimistic thoughts about his growing future finances, to the one single thought of staying alive.

His horse squealed and reared in pain as a shell nicked its flank, nearly unseating him. He stayed on the wildly kicking mount only by the seat of his pants. He paused long enough in his cursing at the horse to yell. 'Let's get the hell out of it!' He hadn't enough men to take on all the guards in this section of the track.

Pablo didn't need any orders to cut and run for it. He was lying only several inches away from a bundle of blasting sticks which, if hit, would not only blow him out of this world but right through the next world he was bound for. He dropped down from the bridge, landing heavily and painfully on his left foot and clawed his way frantically up on to his horse. Chivvied by shells hissing frighteningly close by him, Pablo, heedless of the stabs of pain shooting up his left leg, dug his spurs savagely into his horse's ribs to urge it up the steep sandy bank of the wash, and out of range of the rapidly firing guns.

Al's luck deserted him. Like Pablo, he had a great urge to put as much distance between him and the dynamite. He dropped down into his saddle and as his feet were fumbling for the stirrups he was hit twice in the chest. He slid sideways from the saddle, dead before he hit the floor of the wash.

Pike, further along the wash than Behen, was clear of the field of fire and opened up with his pistol at their attackers as covering fire for his *compadres* to make a break for it. Floyd saw the muzzle-flashes of his pistol and brought his rifle round to fire at a clear target. Pike gave a hoarse, painful grunt, dying fast from a head shot that knocked him off his horse. In a wild tangle of limbs he rolled down the bank of the wash, to meet up with Al in Hell.

'Cease firin'!' Floyd yelled. 'The bastards are pullin' out!'

Joshua heard the sound of horses crashing their way through the brush along the edge of the wash and lowered his rifle, hands trembling, the sweat damp on his brow. He knew they had been lucky. Their attack had caught the dynamiters off guard, confusing them enough for them not to stand and make a fight of it.

'Are we goin' in to see if we've hit any of them, Mr Goad?' he asked.

'No, we're not!' Floyd snapped back, listening, watching intently. 'We've saved the bridge, and that's our task finished here. Soon this place is goin' to be swarmin' with KP guards, shootin' every which way and we don't want to be around when that happens. We just lie low at our camp for the rest of the night.'

Joshua saw Floyd look at the body of the dead guard as they passed by the campfire. Then he turned and looked at him, giving him a glance that froze his blood. He opined that he was catching a glimpse of Floyd T. Goad, the man-hunter.

'Mr Webb,' Floyd said, voice as stony-hard as his face. 'The sonsuvbitches who did that, and the man who's payin' them to do it, are bound for Hell, or they despatch me there first. And that's a God sworn oath, Mr Webb.'

Behen, pounding back to Abilene, was also making some promises, swearing to kill the sons-of-bitches who had scotched his blowing-up of the bridge and gunned down two of his boys. If they weren't already dead they soon would be. The railroad guards would string them up on the handiest tree without bothering to haul them in front of a judge.

Though it had been a get-to-hell-out-of-it-fast situation, Behen reckoned that it had only been two rifles firing on them. And, just as certain, the way they had sneaked up on them, he knew who they were. The railroad trouble-shooters had shown their hands with a vengeance. He had to admit that they were good, kept their presence hidden in Abilene, or wherever else they were holed-up. Somehow the pair had tracked the gang to the bridge, or had made a lucky guess.

Yet Pablo had said that no one had trailed the gang when they had left town, but events had proved that the time to worry how the agents did it was long gone. It had always been a part-personal battle with the railroad, being outwitted and losing two of his boys galled him, making it now a purely personal fight. Turner Lazenby could keep his money. Behen bared his teeth in a wolfish snarl. Once he got back to Abilene he would round up some more men and go on the prod, close-eyeing every son-of-a-bitch in town in a determined attempt to seek out the railroad agents. Any man giving him as much as an unkind look was risking to be shot.

Pablo, clinging tight to his reins, sick-faced with pain from what was only a badly twisted ankle, was also fervently making fearsome promises. Like Behen, he was suffering from loss of face. Like some city greenhorn he had led the gang into an ambush, got Al and Pike shot. To seek out the railroad agents was now a vendetta.

When they were found, their screams would be heard clear all the way to Newton, as he worked on them with his knife. That satisfying thought eased the pain in Pablo's leg somewhat.

The rest of the night passed peacefully at the medicine wagon, Floyd standing the watch. Though he couldn't hear or see anything he knew the railroad guards would be scouring the territory around the bridge for signs of the dynamiters. He guessed that if Phil Spenser was with them he would figure out how things had been played out at the bridge.

When Joshua elbowed himself off his bedroll at daylight he saw Floyd squatting at a blazing fire and smelt coffee brewing. Standing on the wagon, he could see a stretch of the trail through the trees. 'There's riders up there, Mr Goad!' he gasped, coming fully awake.

Floyd grinned up at him. 'I reckoned there would be come daylight,' he said. 'I lit the fire to show them that we're here and Doctor Floyd T. Goad has nothing to hide. They'll likely be comin' down this way to ask us if we heard or seen anything of the men who murdered the guards. We both slept soundly and wouldn't have heard a herd of buffalo stomping through our camp, *comprende,* Mr Webb? Now come on down and have your coffee, we oughta be movin' out soon.'

As he was stepping down from the wagon, Joshua saw one of the riders peel off from the group and come riding towards the trees. He had the urge to take his rifle with him to the fire, they'd already had one brush with the railroad guards and they might turn real nasty this time, but he wouldn't be so bold as to question the old goat's judgement in reading a given situation. If he opined it was sweet-smelling time, then that's what it was. Though he gave a deep sigh of relief as he recognized the rider as the line boss, Mr Spenser.

'Coffee's ready, Phil,' Floyd said. 'You'll be

cravin' for a mug if you've been up on your horse most of the night.'

An ashen-faced, heavy-eyed Spenser swung himself stiffly out of his saddle. 'Floyd,' he said, 'the building of this spur line will see me to an early grave, all the trouble that's hitting it.' He took the mug of coffee Joshua offered him and held it in both hands, warming himself before taking several mouthfuls. 'That's better,' he said. 'I think I'm alive again.' He favoured Floyd and Joshua with a thin smile. 'Thanks for saving my bridge, boys. There was enough dynamite planted on it to have made kindling of it. And you gave me a bonus: you killed two of the bastards, we found their bodies in the wash. My tracker reckons at least another two got away.'

'We're sorry we couldn't save your boys, Phil,' Floyd said. 'But we kinda stumbled in on the sonsuvbitches when they were already at the bridge.'

'The bodies of the dynamiters are on their way to Abilene,' Spenser said. 'The marshal may be able to identify them and who they hung around with. But I fear no one will admit knowing them, other than standing next to them in some saloon or other. Which is fair enough I suppose. During the cattle-trailing season scores of men are moving in and out of town. Are your plans still the same, Floyd?'

'Yeah,' replied Floyd. 'Though you could be takin' one of my suspects back to Abilene slung across his horse, but I doubt it. By what I've heard about Behen he's got more lives than a cook's cat. I'm dropping off Mr Webb, here, at the Carlson spread. Wade's hired him as a ranch-hand. He isn't a KP man: he's just been kinda backin' me up. Without him you would have lost your bridge, Phil.'

'The company appreciates your help, Mr Webb,' Spenser said. 'And being that you're not a regular employee of the railroad I don't see why you should not be entitled to a reward for your action at the bridge. Does that seem right and proper to you, Floyd?'

'Sounds fine to me,' Floyd said. 'The boy sure played his part.'

'I'll send word to you at the Carlson ranch, Mr Webb,' Spenser said, 'when the cash has been deposited in the bank at Abilene. And you take care, Floyd, close-eyeing your suspects. They'll be doing some close-eyeing themselves, trying to find the men who jumped them at the bridge.'

Floyd smiled his empty-faced drummer's smile. 'Who would suspect a dude pedlar of quack medicines of bein' a KP man?'

'Right now, *Doctor* Floyd T. Goad,' Spenser said, stone-faced, 'those sonsuvbitches will be suspecting their own grandmothers.'

'Careful is my middle name, Phil,' Floyd said. 'But bein' that I ain't a store clerk I'm called on sometimes to take risks.' He got to his feet and opened his coat, showing his holstered pistol and the gun sticking out the top of his pants; then came the flick of the wrist and the derringer was in his right fist. And once more Joshua caught a glimpse of the real Floyd T. Goad as the big man's face tightened, losing all its flabbiness, when he spoke again.

'If it is written, as our red brethren put it, that I'm due to go down, Mr Spenser, I don't intend makin' that trip alone.'

Spenser smiled. 'Now I know why you haul your ass around in a wagon, Floyd. There isn't a horse bred that could carry you and all that weight of iron you're toting.' Then, as serious-faced as Floyd he added, 'Now I must get back to my men: we've got two graves to dig. I don't think we'll get more trouble on the line for a while, but I'll still keep the guards patrolling it. To warn them that they'll get another bloody nose if they come this way again. If you need any help, Floyd, you just call on me. It could take more than three guns to regulate this situation.' Spenser hard-eyed Floyd. 'Do you hear, Mr Goad?'

'I hear,' replied Floyd.

'And thank you for your help again, Mr Webb,' Spenser continued. 'And good luck in your new job.' He reached out and gripped Joshua's hand in a firm handshake.

'It's me who should be doin' the thankin'', Mr Spenser,' Joshua said, 'for puttin' me in for the reward.'

'Spend it wisely, Mr Webb,' Spenser said. 'There's good growing land going cheap in Kansas. Crops, corn, whatever, is Kansas's future not cows.' He finished off his coffee and handed back the mug to Joshua. Then, mounting up, and saying a final 'Good Luck', Spenser rode up the rise to the trail.

Floyd tossed the dregs of his coffee on the fire, then with the toes of his boots raked dirt on the hissing embers. 'It's time we were movin' out as well, Mr Webb. Hitch up your buddy to the wagon. I'll get the gear aboard.' He smiled at Joshua. 'In a few hours or so you'll be a genuine cowman.'

Though he was eager to be meeting Miss Beth again, Joshua, in spite of what Floyd had said that he was finished with his services, wasn't too happy leaving him. 'I still feel as though I'm runnin' out on you.'

'You know that's not the way I see it, Mr Webb,' Floyd said. 'And don't you dare think otherwise so I don't want to hear any more of this foolish talk, savvy? Your contract with the Kansas Pacific was terminated at the bridge there.' He grinned at Joshua. 'You'll stay at the Carlson ranch if I have to nail you to one of the barn doors.'

'I'll stay, Mr Goad,' Joshua said. 'But if you get into trouble in Abilene you send for me and I'll watch your back, savvy? After all we're still pards, ain't we?'

'I'll do that, pard,' replied Floyd. Which was as big a lie as he ever had uttered. The kid was well out of the dangerous business of hunting down killers. 'Now get that mule harnessed up to the wagon before the sonuvabitch cottons on to the fact that you're goin' to leave him and takes the sulks and won't move ass.'

Twelve

Turner Lazenby, on his way to the Prairie Dog, could see in his mind's eye the end of his world looming up before him. Behen's fiasco at the bridge, the killing of his two men, meant that the railroad investigators were closer to them than they had supposed. Real close, necktie-party close. Lazenby had come to the conclusion that it was time to call a halt to his attacks on the line, accept the sour fact that the KP would lay its tracks to Newton, and he would go bust.

He still believed that he couldn't be linked in with the dynamiters, even if the marshal identified the two dead raiders as men who worked for him. He hired lots of men on a short-term basis, and the nature of the work they had been taken on for they hadn't to be milksops. After all, he couldn't be expected to check out the background of every man on his payroll to see if they were wanted by the law. That's what he had believed till the mad-assed Behen told him that he wasn't going to damn well throw in his hand.

'The fight's just begun, Lazenby!' he had said back there in his office, eyeballing him across his desk, with a look that scared the hell out of him. 'You can keep your money; I'll destroy the line for free! Mort Behen ain't about to eat crow twice!' Then the crazy son-of-a-bitch had stormed out of his office, leaving him sitting there knowing that if Behen got roped in, he would finger him as the paymaster. He could still be in deep trouble if Behen got killed. He would have to lie through his back teeth to the law to try and convince them that he didn't know about the lawless activities his straw boss was carrying out when not riding shotgun over his freight trains to come out of this mess smelling sweet.

Sick to his stomach with worry, Lazenby

rose from his desk and put on his hat. He looked at his watch. 'Damn it!' he muttered. He should have been at Poker Alice's place half an hour ago to escort her to the card game. By now, he reckoned, she would have set off for the Prairie Dog on her own. By way of apology he would treat her to a bottle of champagne. But Poker Alice was a tetchy female and it could be a while before she got over her huff at him letting her down and allow him back in her bed once more. Not that he was in the mood for bouncing her around. He closed his office door thinking that when Lady Luck left a man she didn't do it by half.

Floyd, on coming into Abilene, noticed that Main Street was quiet. It was as he opined, the wild drovers were on their way back to Texas. Which was a good thing and a bad thing. The good side was he could move around the saloons without the worry of meeting up with the two trail-hands who wanted to gun him down. The not so good was that he couldn't lose himself in the crowded bars. Being a big man he would be instantly noticed walking into a saloon by men who, by now, had cottoned on to the fact that a KP man was in the territory, and were raising a lot of sweat trying to find him.

He had to work real hard at his oily-smiling, pill-pedlar drummer image or Floyd T. Goad could be investigating his last case. With that disturbing thought in his mind, Floyd drove the wagon into the livery barn.

Within half an hour he was walking along the boardwalk heading for the Prairie Dog, hoping to get his first assaying looks at Mr Turner Lazenby and Mr Mort Behen, the one time Missouri guerilla. He had thoroughly checked his three pistols, feeling as ready to meet any emergency as any man stepping into the unknown could. Only to discover that his preparations were found wanting.

Sam Cassidy hadn't left town with the rest of the crew. He had stayed in Abilene till he met up with the big fat dude who had put a slug in him, and the young blue-belly kid who had shot his *compadre*, Lars, real bad. Lars was now lying in the back of the cook's wagon on the trail to Texas, bleeding inside him. The betting amongst the crew was that Lars would be ready for planting before they crossed the Red.

The law hadn't been told of the shooting. Justice, Texan style, was a more personal business. An Old Testament eye for an eye, getting even justice. Administered by Colonel Colt and Judge Lynch.

Cassidy could hardly believe his luck when he saw the big dude coming along the street towards him. He smiled. His luck was really riding high, the dude was on his own, his sidekick, the kid, was nowhere in sight. It would be an even match. Cassidy's smile broadened. More even for him when he sneaked up to the son-of-a-bitch and stuck a big .45 in his side.

Poker Alice was in a bad temper. Lazenby had stood her up and here she was having to walk to the Prairie Dog all by herself. That wasn't in keeping with what she reckoned a woman who had high hopes to be seen as a fine lady had to put up with. The fine ladies she had read about in the Eastern magazines never walked anywhere without being escorted by a fine-looking man. While she had to admit that Turner Lazenby could be in no way classed as a fine-looking man, in fact lately he was becoming a real pain in the ass, he was a big man in the town. Townspeople touched their hats to him and addressed him as Mr Lazenby. And that's what Poker Alice craved for; respectability. She would give half of what was lying in her strongbox in the cathouse to have folk raise their hats to her. Greeting her with a smile and a 'Good day, Miss Alicia', instead of, 'Hiya, Poker Alice, got any fresh girls in the cathouse?'

She might run a whorehouse but it was the cleanest in the territory. Why she had even entertained a former state governor in her place before he became the number one in the state. It was a business she ran and, unlike some of the town's businesses, no one got short-changed. Poker Alice's black mood suddenly vanished and her heart gave several unexplained leaps. The big pill doctor was standing across the street in conversation with a man whose right arm was in a sling, a trail-hand, she thought. As he came closer to them she saw that only the Texan was doing the talking. And by his scowling look it was anything but sweet words he was spouting.

Floyd, his mind occupied with how things could develop, didn't sense his danger till something hard pressed into his back and the hissed warning of, 'Make a move for a gun, pilgrim, and I'll plug you right here. You've shot your last Texan.'

Floyd stood still and the man stepped round to face him. Floyd, he told himself, this is what comes of being soft-hearted. You should have downed the bastard for good instead of just winging him.

Floyd grunted with pain as Cassidy thrust the pistol barrel in his belly. He did some desperate, rapid, life-saving calculations and came up with the same depressing answers, he had no chance at all to pull out one of his guns, including the derringer, before the Texan put a load in his guts.

'Now you and me will take a stroll, looking nice and friendly-like, to that alley back there,' Cassidy said. 'And I'll finish off the business you started by backin' up that Yankee kid. I'm only sorry I can't shoot the kid as well, but I'll find the bastard and send him on his way to meet up with you. It'll kinda even up things for poor Lars who ain't expected to make it to Texas.'

While Floyd knew he had made a mistake by just wounding the Texan, the trail-hand was making a bigger error of judgement. Floyd's basic rule was that if it's in your heart to kill a man, you do just that, by yanking out your pistol and shooting him down. Don't waste time yapping about your intentions to his face. All was not yet lost, he thought hopefully, he was still breathing.

Poker Alice saw the gun the Texan was

holding on the big dude. In all of her life in the frontier and railhead towns she had witnessed many gunfights and shoot-outs between two men, even between rival cattle crews and had taken the view that if wild-asses were obsessed with the urge to shoot holes in each other it was no one's business but theirs, or the law's. This time it was different. Although she had only seen the big dude twice she felt some sort of attraction towards him and she didn't want to see him shot down like a dog without the chance of defending himself, whatever his disagreement with the Texan was.

Poker Alice quickened her pace till she was about to pass by them then suddenly turned and pushed her way in front of the Texan. She looked up at Floyd, smiling.

'Why, Doc,' she said. 'I didn't expect to see you back in town so soon.'

She heard the Texan behind her dirty-mouthing away, trying to elbow her out of his way. Floyd, the look of surprise still on his face at a whorehouse madam coming to his aid, didn't waste the chance she had given him. He yanked out his shoulder Colt and towering above Poker Alice reached over her and brought it down hard on the trail-hand's head. Soundlessly, Cassidy crumpled to the ground, out to the wide.

Floyd smiled with grateful relief as he slipped the gun back into its holster. 'Ma'am,' he said, 'you sure got me out of a tight situation. Thanks.' He touched the brim of his hat. 'Doctor Floyd T. Goad is pleased to make your acquaintance, ma'am.'

'I'm Pok–, Miss Alicia Sands,' Poker Alice said. 'I run the best cathouse in the territory. I saw that the Texan had you by the ba–' Poker Alice suddenly thought that 'Miss Alicia' wouldn't use a suchlike word in front of a man whom she hardly knew. 'I saw that he had an unfair advantage over you.' She sweet-smiled. 'I kinda stepped in to even things up somewhat.'

'And I'm right grateful you did, Miss Alicia,' Floyd said. 'The sonuvabitch was about to see me well and truly dead.' Then he did some sweet-smiling of his own. 'I believe I saw you earlier on in the week when I was leaving town. And if you don't mind me sayin' so, you looked quite purty. You're even purtier dressed up in that fine gown, Miss Alicia.'

Poker Alice surprised herself by coming over all hot and cold, and her heart began playing her up. Sweet Jesus, she thought, getting control of her unusual emotions, I'll be fluttering my eyelids at Mr Floyd T. Goad soon like some love-sick kid. She gave Floyd a whorehouse madam's beady-eyed look but could see nothing oily and false in his smile. And she also noticed that he met her scrutinizing gaze with a steeliness in his eyes no drummer she ever had dealings with showed.

'You must pay me a call before you leave town, Mr Goad,' she said. 'That's if it ain't against any beliefs you may hold about visiting cathouses.'

'My only beliefs, Miss Alicia,' Floyd replied, 'is that life bein' so short as it is, a man should get his pleasures when and where he can find them. Now I reckon I should haul this *hombre* along to the marshal's office and explain to him what happened.'

'Was he trying to rob you, Mr Goad?' Poker Alice asked.

Floyd shook his head. 'Naw, I had a brush with him and some of his buddies when I first came to town. I was forced to put a slug in his shoulder. It seems that he's a man who holds a grudge a while.'

By hell, the Texan is entitled to bear a grudge against the man who shot him, Poker Alice opined. She thought the big man was ribbing her, but although he was still smiling the humour had gone out of it. And Poker Alice, who had slept with *pistoleros*, white and brown, and other similar hardcases, couldn't stop the icy chills running up and down her spine. If Mr Goad was a drummer she would enter a nunnery. She knew about the trouble on the spur line and began to wonder if the big man was in Abilene for that reason. The railroad was offering a big reward to anyone who brought in the dynamiters. That sort of money, she knew, would attract the bounty hunters, men desperate enough for the crock of gold at the rainbow's end to risk their lives trying to bring in the wanted men.

'If the old goat gets awkward, Mr Goad,' Poker Alice said, 'you must mention my name.' She smiled. 'Tell him I won't let him fool around with Big Kate the next time he comes into my place.'

'I'll do that,' replied Floyd. 'And I'll definitely pay your establishment a visit when my business is finished here.' If things went bad for him, he thought, the only place he could be visiting would be Boot Hill, on a one-way trip.

'I'll look forward to seeing you there, Mr Goad,' Poker Alice said. 'Ask for me when you arrive. Now I must go, my friends will be waiting for me in the Prairie Dog.' Poker Alice turned and continued on her way to the poker game. Not sure if she had made a fool of herself by fluttering her eyelids at the big, mysterious Doctor Floyd T. Goad.

Floyd watched her swaying-ass walk. He grinned. Miss Alicia was certainly no chicken but she still had what made a man's blood run hot and wild. Even an over-the-hill old fart like him. All the old fart had to do to enjoy humping Miss Alicia was to stay alive. Which wouldn't be easy. The dynamiters would also want to stay above ground. Pulling his gaze away from Miss Alicia, Floyd bent down and picked up the inert body of the Texan and hoisted it over his left shoulder. He hoped the marshal's lust for Big Kate was strong enough for him to be persuaded to keep the Texan under lock and key for a few days at least. The trouble which lay ahead of him was as much as he could handle without having a revenge-seeking Texan stalking him as well.

Thirteen

Floyd sat at a table where he had an unrestricted view of the door and the bar, gimlet-eyeing the drinkers already in the saloon, and the steady flow of customers coming into the Prairie Dog, trying to pick out a man who, he opined, had the cut of a Missouri ex-brush boy. A cut, he uncharitably thought, Abilene being a tough, wide-open trail town, fitted almost every drinker at the bar.

At a table closer to the bar, Floyd saw the cathouse madam playing cards with three store-suited men. She caught his gaze and smiled at him. Floyd gave her one of his beaming grins. Miss Alicia, or Poker Alice, or whatever name she fancied calling herself, had just helped him out again. In the marshal's office he had unceremoniously dumped the still unconscious Texan in a chair.

'I'm Doctor Floyd T. Goad, a patent medicine specialist,' he began, in a sky pilot's preaching voice. 'That Texan sonuva-bitch pulled a gun on me and demanded my roll. What sort of law do you run in this burg, Marshal, when hold-up men can practise their thieving trade in broad daylight? But Floyd T. Goad ain't a man who is easily caught short. I cold-cocked the bastard. Now I know that tryin' to rob a citizen ain't a capital offence like robbin' a bank or heistin' a stage is, but even so I reckon he's due for a spell in one of your cells.'

Marshal Blunt's grey longhorn bristled under a bulbous, red-veined nose. He didn't take kindly to the big, moon-faced dude barging into his office telling him how he should run his town. The carpet-bagging son-of-a-bitch should be run out of town for trying to con the townsfolk to part with their hard-earned cash for the quack cures

134

he was selling. And as for jailing the injured trail-hand he was seriously contemplating throwing the smooth-talking bastard himself in the cooler for bodily assault.

Floyd's eyes narrowed, seeing in the marshal's face that he wasn't about to judicate in his favour. 'I have a witness to prove that the Texan drew on me, unprovoked. A Miss Alicia.'

'Miss Alicia? Who the hell is she?' the marshal asked.

'Why she's the cathouse owner, Marshal,' replied Floyd, slightly puzzled. Thinking that the sweet-assed madam had been only joshing him regarding her influence over the marshal, even to go as far as to give him a false name.

'Oh, you mean Poker Alice,' said the marshal.

'Whoever,' replied Floyd. Then, bland-faced, he added, 'Miss Alicia said I had to tell you that if you were to prove uncooperative she would see to it that Big Kate wouldn't be around the next time you paid a visit to the cathouse.'

Floyd saw the marshal's anger drain from his face, becoming white and drawn. Big Kate sure had some pull, Floyd thought. She must be one hell of a whore. Maybe he would get the time to enjoy her talents.

Marshal Blunt pictured the big-breasted Kate lying in his arms. God, he thought, he would rather cut off his right leg than forego that pleasure.

'Miss … Poker Alicia said that,' Marshal Blunt said, not looking directly at Floyd.

Floyd twisted the knife in. 'Her exact words, Marshal.'

With his gaze still directed on his desk the marshal said, 'Yeah, well, m'be on second thoughts a spell back there in the cells will show the trail-hand that the law in Abilene stomps hard on robbin' sonsuvbitches.'

'Thanks, Marshal,' said Floyd. 'The next time I see Miss Alicia I'll tell her how co-operative you've been.' He left the marshal's office somewhat eased in his mind now that his backtrail was clear.

Floyd swung his gaze back on to the poker table. The player in his shirt-sleeves with a heavy gold watch chain hanging across a fancy patterned vest raised a hand. Floyd saw one of the barkeeps come from behind the bar balancing a tray which held a large bottle of wine and four glasses and brought it to the table. Floyd's nostrils dilated, the trail had hotted up again. He had got his first sighting of his chief suspect, Mr Turner Lazenby. Without appearing to be too nosy he gave the freight owner a longer, serious look.

He saw Lazenby snarl something at the barkeep as he placed the drinks down on the table and made to pour out the wine, then wave him away with a sharp dismissive gesture. By the expression on his face and his angry actions, Floyd opined that Turner Lazenby had a lot chewing away at him. He hoped the freight owner was feeling the strain on his nerves running in tandem with killers.

Whatever else he was, Lazenby was no

fool. He must know that the KP would use all its resources to track down the dynamiters, and that it would be only a matter of time before they were successful. Lazenby, Floyd thought, was sitting there getting belly ulcers trying to sweat it out.

Just then, Floyd's attention was drawn to four men pushing their way through the swing doors. The leading man had a mean-eyed stomping-man's face and favoured the wearing of two pistols; one in a holster on his right hip, the other, like his, pushed in his pants top, for the fast action style of the Missourian brush boys. Floyd's nostrils flared bull like again. He had no doubts that he was checking out Mr Mort Behen.

The man closest to the Missourian, a 'breed, Floyd reckoned, wore only one gun, holstered across his belly, butt outwards cataloguing him as a cross-draw man. Floyd was more interested in the big bladed knife the mixed-blood carried in a bead-work sheath. That knife, he thought, grimly, in the hands of its stone-faced owner, was capable of cutting some poor unsuspecting guard's throat.

It gave Floyd some satisfaction that Behen's face held the same pinched look as his boss's. The Missourian wouldn't have had much sleep since his failed raid on the bridge trying to figure out why things went wrong. And who and where were the men who had made it go all wrong and cost him two men. Floyd knew he hadn't to sit on his ass, smug-faced at his success so far against the gang, or the sons-of-bitches would finally get round to checking him out and the 'breed could find work for his big blade.

The four men bellied up to the bar and Floyd began to figure out his next moves to bring the dynamiters to justice; to bring them in alive to face the hangman, or bring them in lying face down across their horses, tarp-wrapped and dead.

He could go straight for Lazenby, him being the weak link in the operation. Force him, at pistol point if needs be, to write out and sign a paper implicating himself in the raids. Then again, Lazenby might not be easily broken if cornered and before he knew otherwise, Lazenby's lawyers would have him in court for harassing a prominent citizen of Abilene.

His other option, he hardly dare call it a plan, was to keep a wary eye on Behen and the knife-toting 'breed. Trail them when they left town on what he judged wasn't legitimate freight-line business. He could also ask Silas Black for men, but an ex-guerrilla would soon spot a posse dogging him, so his roping in of the whole gang had to be curtailed somewhat. If he caught them in the act of sabotaging the line, the final proof, he would shoot Behen. His killing would put an end to the dynamiting. If his luck ran high he would put the 'breed where he rightly belonged, stoking up the fires of Hell. The rest of Behen's boys could then be rounded up by Marshal Blunt and his deputies.

Floyd gave an inner grin. It was almost a plan after all. He also thought that he had seen all he could here and decided to go back to the wagon, see to Ulysses then catch a good night's sleep. Maybe the last he would get for quite a spell; maybe the last one ever if Behen discovered who he really was.

Poker Alice had been doing some keen-eyeing of her own. Twice she had caught sight of what she believed was the genuine Floyd T. Goad. Once when he had looked across at Turner Lazenby, and again when Behen and his wild boys came into the saloon. For a few seconds his Hicksville face mask had slipped, Indianing over to become as fierce as any border ruffian's. He had the smell of big trouble hanging over him. Shooting and killing trouble. Trouble that could get the big man dead. Which was a shame, Poker Alice thought, she would have liked Mr Goad to keep his promise and pay her a call.

Poker Alice was convinced now that Mr Goad was here in Abilene because of the trouble on the KP spur line. Turner

Lazenby and Behen were involved in those raids on the line. She had no difficulty believing that Behen was tied in with the dynamiters, that son-of-a-bitch was capable of blowing up his own grandmother if someone made it worth his while to do so.

It took a while for her to accept that Lazenby, her bed and social companion, could have a hand in out-and-out law-breaking activities, including killings. Yet accept it she did, albeit reluctantly. Lazenby had more to lose than the other business-men in town, and lately he had been showing it in his face and manner towards her. What made her sure that Lazenby had crossed the line was the strong feeling that Mr Floyd T. Goad didn't seem a man who made wild guesses. If he smelt a rat, in this case a whole parcel of rats, she would take his word for it. When she glanced across at his table to see if she could read further confirmation of her views in his face, the big man was on his way out of the saloon.

Before he dropped off to sleep on the hard

boards of the wagon bed, Floyd thought of Joshua and the pleasure he would be enjoying being close to the sweet-smiling Miss Beth. And of the delights he would get if lying with the big-breasted Miss Alicia. Floyd sighed. The only night companion he had was the flea-bag, Ulysses, tethered to the wagon, snorting and snuffling, ornery as always, even when resting. What the hell did a man who travelled with death at his side expect? The rocking-chair on the front stoop and a warm-hearted woman to tend to his every need? In the profession he had chosen to earn his keep he was lucky Ulysses stayed with him.

Another two men joined Behen and the rest of the gang at the bar, bringing the scowling-faced Missourian the same negative news of their lack of success locating the whereabouts of the KP agents or any likely *hombre* who could be a railroad man. Behen thumped the bar top with his fist so fiercely that the whiskey bottle and glasses bounced inches in the air.

'The bastards are out there!' he snarled. 'We ain't been lookin' in the right places, that's all. Who the hell shot the boys at the bridge, Injuns?'

'We checked the livery barn, boss,' one of the newcomers said. 'But according to the owner no stranger has ridden into town this past week. If they have they ain't boarded their mounts with him. And there ain't no way we can check out all the men who came by rail to the town, if the bastards were passin' themselves off as cattle buyers.'

Behen cursed. He had been expecting too much. The KP agents had proved by their ambush at the bridge they were no greenhorns. Did he expect them to come riding into town wearing big signs telling everyone who they were? No, he thought, the sons-of-bitches would be holed-up some place near, watching and waiting, biding their time for him to go out on another raid. Behen began cursing again, then suddenly stopped as he heard Lou say, 'The livery barn owner did mention that a pill doctor was in town, his wagon is at the rear of his barn right now.'

Behen straightened up from the bar. 'Pill doctor?' he said. He close-eyed Lou, brain working at full speed.

'Yeah, a big dude, selling quack medicines and ointments,' Lou replied. 'The barn owner reckons he pulled into town earlier on in the week then left by the Newton trail. A young kid was with him drivin' the wagon. And as I said, the dude's back in town, though without the kid. He keeps his mule company by sleepin' in the wagon.'

'Now who the hell is there to sell pills to along that trail, Lou?' Behen said. 'There ain't but a coupla small ranches out there. And the Irish at the rail camp ain't pill-swallowin' men, are they?' Behen bared his teeth into a fearsome smile. He had a gut-feeling they had found the railroad agents. The sons-of-bitches had been using the perfect cover, even sleeping holed-up. 'Pablo,' he said, 'when it quietens down you take Lou and Nick and have words with this dude doctor. Check him out real good. If he smells like a lawman bring him along to the freight depot and I'll pass the time of day with him.'

Pablo grinned, there was no lamplight shining through the open front of the wagon. The dude was in for a surprise awakening. 'You over the back of the wagon, Lou,' he said softly. 'Nick, stay loose in case the kid shows up.' He drew out his big knife. 'I'll step inside the wagon and give the dude his early mornin' call.'

Ulysses' ears pricked up and his jaundiced red-eyed glare followed a dark shape moving slowly towards him. Lou cursed, he couldn't get close to the tailgate of the wagon, a big stinking-to-high-heaven mule was tied up there. He jabbed his pistol barrel into the animal's ribs. 'Move ass, you dumb critter!' he growled.

Ulysses, a maverick among his own kind, spread his natural-born bad temper to cover humans as well, especially those who caused him pain. His lips drew back baring big yellow teeth in a snarling neigh as he kicked out with both back legs. Lou felt twin cannonballs hitting him in the chest, caving in his ribcage as he was sent flying backwards through the air, landing on the ground in a crumpled heap, choking to death on his own blood that poured out of his mouth in a dark flood.

Floyd, by nature of his profession, slept with one eye open, heard Ulysses voicing his anger, and the sickening thud of iron-shod hooves hitting something soft and vulnerable. He sprang to his feet as quickly and smoothly as a man half his age and weight. Sweeping up one of the Colts from a box top, and automatically thumbing back the hammer, he stepped to the front of the wagon. For one fleeting second he thought that if it was the livery barn owner who had tangled with Ulysses, then he would owe him, or his widow, an apology. And Ulysses was due for a piece of name-calling.

He drew back the tarp cover and stepped

cautiously outside, to peer eagle-eyed in the darkness. He suddenly gave out a gasp of pain as he felt a burning, stabbing sensation at the back of his right shoulder that caused him to sag at the knees. In the quick movement of the 'border shift' he threw the pistol into his left hand before the numbness of his wound deadened his right arm and fired, almost in blind panic, in the direction from where he guessed the knife in his shoulder had been thrown.

Pablo howled like a kicked cur dog and clapped a hand to the bloody shreds of flesh that had been his right ear. Knowing that they had lost the edge, and hearing that something unpleasant had also happened to Lou, Pablo quickly decided that it was looking-after-number-one time and beat a stumbling footed, but hasty retreat out of the yard. Floyd gave a weak, agonized grin. Two down, and still on his feet, just. A pistol flashed and roared away to his left, its load ripping through the side post close by his head. This time he had a clearer target.

Gritting his teeth at the pain that was threatening to make him black out, he triggered off a shot slightly to the left of where he had seen the muzzle flash.

Floyd thought he heard a body falling heavily to the ground, but he couldn't be sure, the wound was making him hazy-headed, dulling all his senses. Half-crouched, face twisted in a defiant, last-chance stance, he waited for the next shot, the killing shot. His luck was still riding high; no further shots were fired at him from the darkness. There must have only been three of the sons-of-bitches. Though Floyd was well aware that it wasn't the time to stand and crow about his good fortune.

By now the knife-wielding 'breed whom he had heard running away would be telling Behen the score and he reckoned that when they came the next time, the Missourian would be coming in with them. One mule and a man with a knife stuck in his back, he couldn't reach to pull out, would have no chance holding them off till the local law got up off its ass to come and see what the shooting was all about.

It was time to seek a hole to crawl into, to lie low, lick his wounds, so that he could fight another day. Behen was calling the shots now. And the bastard was thorough. They could have only come for him on suspicion alone; that meant Behen was checking out all recent visitors to town. His edge had gone; it was open warfare from now on in.

Floyd stepped away from the wagon gingerly, wincing with pain every movement he made. He could feel the warm stickiness of blood trickling down his back. The knife was acting as a wound plug and if it slipped out, the blood would flow more freely. While he opined that he wouldn't bleed to death if that happened, the loss of blood would weaken him and, as strong as he was, he would pass out before he could get to a safe haven and have the wound attended to.

And he had decided on a refuge: Miss Alicia's cathouse, if she was agreeable to having a man on the run from a bunch of killing men and all the trouble that could bring her. Miss Alicia had come to his aid once, he was hoping that she would put herself out again on his behalf.

He walked to the rear of the wagon before heading for the cathouse to check on Ulysses and, with pistol fisted and cocked, to make sure that the mule's victim was no further threat to him. He patted Ulysses soothingly on the neck as he saw a dark, still, crumpled heap several feet away from the mule.

'Ulysses,' he said, 'if you weren't so plain dumb ugly I'd swear I'd kiss you. You saved my neck, that's for sure. I'm beholden to you. When this little upset's over I'll buy you a sack of the best feed money can buy.'

Ulysses gave a soft, deep-throated growling sound and flexed his back legs. Floyd managed a grin. 'You bloodthirsty critter,' he said. 'The war's over for you, I'll take you over to the barn and you stay there and try not to be so mean-tempered and get me a bad name, savvy *compadre?*' He began a one-handed task of loosening the tethering rope when he saw the bobbing light of a hand-held storm lantern coming towards him. Floyd swung round his pistol, taking up the first pressure on the trigger. His screwed up nerves heightened the pain of his wound before he recognized the voice as that of the stable owner shouting, 'What the hell's the shootin' about!'

'It's all over!' Floyd yelled back.

The stable owner came up close to Floyd. 'I heard the shootin', then I saw the 'breed who runs with Mort Behen skoot past my barn as though his ass was on fire. By the lantern light I could see the blood runnin' down his face as though the bastard had been scalped. Then comin' across here I almost fell over another *hombre* with the back of his head blown off!' The stable owner raised his lantern higher. 'Holy Moses!' he gulped. 'Is that another body?'

'Yeah,' replied Floyd. 'But it ain't my doin'. Ulysses is entitled to notch up that one.'

'My yard is bein' turned into a battlefield!' the stable owner said angrily. 'What the hell's goin' on?'

'I guess it's only fair you should be told,' Floyd replied. 'I'm a railroad agent here in Abilene to investigate the sabotaging of the new spur line. Those two lying here are, like the 'breed, part of Behen's gang, the men responsible for the trouble and came to put me out of circulation. Now I'd be grateful if you could contact Silas Black, the KP district boss, and tell him I'm OK and that the case is now wide open. Tell him it's between me and Behen, he'll understand. And I'd be obliged if you could take my mule into your barn, the KP will honour any bill you present for his keep, and you'd better keep your head down, for I reckon before long Behen himself with some more of his bully boys will come boilin' in here to hunt me down. And they'll all be triggered up to shoot at their own shadows.'

The stable owner cast nervous glances around him. He wanted no part in the trouble the railroad dude was involved in. The sooner he was out of his yard, the faster his stomach would settle down. He felt like physically pushing him out if the big bastard didn't look such a hard-faced *hombre*. Though that didn't stop him quickly mentally calculating how much he would rake in selling the KP agent's mule and wagon. If Mort Behen was out for his blood the dude was living on borrowed time.

'I'll see Silas,' he said, 'and pass on what you've told me. And don't fret about your mule, he'll be fed and watered regularly.'

'Thanks,' replied Floyd, thinking that the stable owner had better see to Ulysses' needs or he'll end up going head first through his barn roof. Giving Ulysses a final pat, Floyd turned and walked out of the yard. He had drawn the sons-of-bitches out into the open. He had all the proof he needed that Behen and his wild bunch were the dynamiters, the knife in his back was a painful confirmation of that. Maybe still not enough for Silas Black to put them up in front of a circuit judge, but enough for Judge Colt to dispense his one-way-ticket-to-Hell kind of justice on them.

'Well I'll be danged,' the stable owner breathed. By the light from his lantern he could swear that he had seen a knife sticking out the big dude's shoulder. He did some more fast reckoning up, just what he was going to buy with the cash he would get for his effects.

Floyd made his tortuous way to the whorehouse with as much urgency as his rapidly weakening strength could force his legs along. With only two loads left in his pistol, he would be hard pressed to hold off a wild dog. But that's the way it had to be. He hadn't the strength to climb back into the wagon for his other Colt.

Fourteen

Turner Lazenby, face looking as though the Grim Reaper had tapped him on the shoulder, was in his office only part listening to Behen telling him of his suspicions that the quack pill doctor was a KP agent, and how that cut-throat Pablo was bringing him back to the freight depot for questioning.

Lazenby was long past sleeping, long way past spending the night pleasuring Poker Alice. He had even excused himself from escorting her back to the cathouse on the grounds that he had to oversee some urgent freight loaded on to the wagons. Now, by what he was hearing from the mad-assed Behen, he would never sleep again till the law came and dragged him to the jail, prior to stringing him up.

If the railroad agent was brought back

156

here he would never leave the depot alive. Behen would make sure of that. The deaths at the cutting had upset him, but they had been forty miles away; the agent would be killed in his office. Party to cold-blooded murder this close almost made him throw-up over his desk. His foolish belief that he could fight the Kansas Pacific, he thought bitterly, had resulted in him digging his own grave.

'Do you think it's wise bringing the agent here, Behen?' he asked. 'Someone might notice him being brought to the depot. And that could bring the law down on us. The railroad might suspect that we're the men behind the dynamiting; we don't want to give them the proof to be able to arrest us.'

Behen didn't give a damn if the KP brought in the army to rope them in. He had already decided to pull out of Abilene once he had evened up the score with their agent and raid the line the way they used to attack the Kansas Free-Staters' homesteads during the war from bases that were always moved around. And he would let the whole territory know that it was an old Missouri brush boy and his gang who were hitting the railroad where it hurt. That, Behen thought proudly, would get him a rep as fearful to the Union as 'Bloody' Bill Anderson and his guerrilla fighters had during the war.

He fish-eyed Lazenby. The way the chicken-livered son-of-a-bitch looked, he had already quit the fight but hadn't the balls to tell him. Then Behen came to another decision. Before they pulled out he would shoot Lazenby, then there would be no chance of him smooth-talking his way out of his part in the raids by heaping all the blame on him. The way he saw it a man had to accept losing a fight without quitting the battle.

The bursting open of the office door and the sight of the wild-eyed Pablo, blood turning his face into a bizarre red mask, brought Lazenby a mite of comfort. He hoped that the 'breed had a fatal head wound. On looking closer he saw that he was only minus an ear. Painful enough for the 'breed, he thought, but more painful to the 'breed would be the fact that he hadn't brought the KP agent with him. While it wasn't something to shout from the barn roof, Lazenby felt that he had stepped back a few inches from his grave.

'The bastard got away!' Pablo cried, before Behen could ask him what had gone wrong in the stable yard. 'And I stuck my knife into the asshole's shoulder to cripple him!'

'Where's the boys?' Behen snapped, thinking that if a man wanted a job doing right it was no good sending in the hired help. With the blood spattered over his face he looked like a war-painted-up Comanche buck all set to ride out on a killing raid. Upset him any further by querying his courage, the wild bastard would gut-shoot him.

'I dunno, dead I reckon, if they ain't here,' Pablo growled. 'I'm lucky I ain't lyin' back there.'

Behen had lived a life of raiding and killing, and avoiding being killed. A knife-edge existence in which a man had to think well ahead of the opposition to stay above ground. Fretting over things that had gone wrong was valuable time being wasted. And it was time to tie up loose ends. He gave Pablo a significant look, pointing with his chin at Lazenby, and the open safe at the back of his desk. He would have shot the chicken-livered bastard himself, but a killing would calm down the 'breed, take his mind off the pain of his chewed-up ear.

'You see to your wound,' he said. 'I'll get the rest of the boys ready to ride out, loaded for bear. We'll have a quick look round the livery barn for the pill doctor. If he's got your knife in him he could be lyin' in some nearby alley. If we don't find him we'll pick us another day to put paid to the sonuvabitch. I'll see you before I go, Lazenby,' he added, lyingly.

'Yeah,' mumbled Lazenby, too dumb-minded by events that had turned his world upside down to do no more than let fate, whatever it had in store for him, show itself. Thankful that Behen, by pulling out of Abilene, couldn't heap any more trouble on him. He looked up at the sound of breaking glass and saw that Pablo had pulled a cloth off a side table, scattering the framed photographs on it and was wrapping it round his head as a makeshift bandage. Then he jerked up straight in his seat with alarm and gazed with a disbelieving, horrified look at the cold-smiling Pablo, and the pistol pointing at him. He managed to mouth a strangled-voiced, 'No!' before the 'breed's single shot shattered his brain.

The impact of the close-range shot thrust Lazenby hard up against the back of his chair, uptilting it, spilling him on to the floor. Pablo came round the desk and heaved the body from the front of the safe with the toe of his boot. Kneeling down, he began to stuff the tied-up bundles of dollar bills that lay in neat piles on the shelves into his jacket pockets. He glanced at Lazenby's body as he got to his feet. His good feelings vanished and his face became all *bronco* red again. When the son-of-a-bitch he had knifed was as dead as Lazenby, and by his own hand, only then would he be really happy.

Behen heard the faint crack of a pistol shot. He smiled. A potential turncoat had been eliminated, and he had got himself rich in the process.

Floyd made it safely to the whorehouse without being shot at by shadowy figures from dark alleys, though he felt as though some ranch hand had stamped him with a branding-iron and he had difficulty in seeing straight. He opined that for a man on the wrong side of fifty, and being wounded and all, he had done well to make it this far. Old Ulysses would be proud of him.

He had no idea what time it was; it was even hard for him to recollect what day it was. He knew that it must be in the early hours, the saloons and the bars were all shuttered up. He was pleased to see lights behind the drapes at some of the windows of the cathouse. Stumbling about the building in the dark looking for Miss Alicia's room was asking to be taken for a prowler and inviting a load of buckshot in his hide. Floyd gave a painful twist of a grin. Though, he opined, in the state he must look, with the left side of his coat stiffening up with dried blood, he would throw a scare into her walking in on her in broad daylight.

Poker Alice was sitting at her dressing-table, idly brushing her hair, thinking about what she had observed in the saloon, of big trouble brewing up between Lazenby, Behen and the quack doctor, Floyd T. Goad. She hadn't altered her earlier assessment of Turner Lazenby, that he was involved in the dynamiting of the new line. It was written all over his face that he expected something nasty coming his way, pretty damn soon. And in no way was she taken in by the city-dressed, moon-faced dude passing himself off as a pill doctor. Mr

Floyd T. Goad, she knew for sure, was the *hombre* who had put that pinched-ass look on Lazenby's face.

Poker Alice felt no sympathy towards Lazenby, a man whose company she enjoyed, in and out of bed. Lazenby, she thought, was about to pay the bill for being in cahoots with a murdering son-of-a-bitch, like Mort Behen. She had once read somewhere about having a long spoon if eating with the Devil. She wouldn't even sit down in the same eating-house as Behen. It was no-good getting all het up over events that weren't really her business, Poker Alice thought. Though she would like to see Mr Floyd T. Goad come through the trouble still breathing and able to move around.

The big downstairs lounge was only dimly lit when Floyd entered the cathouse. He caught a glimpse of a man sitting in a chair just inside the room, hat pulled over his eyes, and a shotgun laid across his knees. Floyd tagged him as a bouncer. If he woke him up he would get that load of buckshot in his ass for sure.

Slowly, painfully, Floyd climbed the stairs, listening hard for any sudden break in the bouncer's heavy snoring. On making it to the top, he was forced to take a breather. He was almost home and dry. He reckoned he would live to give the 'breed his knife back, along with a couple of better-aimed Colt shells to put an end to his killing days. That was if Miss Alicia didn't have him slung out in the street on his neck.

The lamps were lit along the corridor and Floyd saw that the door nearest him was marked 'Private', in gold letters, and the room faced Main Street. Miss Alicia's room, he hoped. He also noticed a strip of light shining under the bottom of the door, so, if he had guessed right, she could still be awake. He slipped the pistol back into the top of his pants. Walking in on her with a gun fisted could see her yelling out that she was being robbed, and two shotgun loads would be heading his way. A knife in his back was all his constitution could take, catching a shotgun blast would mean that the 'breed would have the last laugh.

Through her dressing-table mirror, Poker Alice saw the door slowly opening. Her face hardened in resolute, manly lines as she lowered her brush on to the table and quietly opened a drawer and took out a small pistol that lay on top of her folded clothes. She then swung round on her chair, facing the door, and cocked the pistol. If the sneaky bastard was looking for easy pickings, she angrily thought, he was due for a big shock. And she would have hard words with Otis, one of her bouncers, for allowing the intruder to reach the private rooms unchallenged.

The door opened wide, and Poker Alice smiled. The big dude was paying her a call. Then as Floyd stepped, tangle-footed, into the room she saw a sunken-eyed, pale, blood-drained face. She leapt to her feet, her welcoming smile replaced by a look of concern as she put out an arm to steady him. She sobbed a horrified, 'Oh my God!'

on seeing the knife embedded in his shoulder. 'Sit down, sit down, Mr Goad, before you fall down!' She guided him to a straight-backed chair and helped him to sit.

Floyd smelt her perfume, felt the heavy softness of big loose-hanging breasts as he eased himself down in the chair. Poker Alice saw a bright spot of light appear for a moment at the back of his blank, unfocused eyes.

'You old horn-dog,' she said softly to herself. 'You ain't got the strength to even think of rollin' around the bed with me.' Then louder she said, 'Now tell me how the hell you came to have a knife stickin' in your back, Mr Goad?'

'I work for the railroad, Miss Alicia,' replied Floyd, his voice sounding as though it didn't belong to him. 'Passin' myself off as a pill doctor was only a cover. I'm trackin' down the gang that's been sabotagin' the new spur line. I found them, but the sonsuvbitches also found me, as you can see. Well, bein' in a kinda desperate situation, and bein' that you've helped me out once before, this was the only place I could think of coming to for help. I just hope they ain't trailed me here. I don't want to sicc the KP's trouble on you, Miss Alicia.' Floyd tried to get back on to his feet.

Poker Alice laid a gentle but restraining hand on his arm. 'You stay put, Mr Goad,' she said. 'Trouble and me ain't strangers. And I guess that the sonsuvbitches you're talkin' about are Mort Behen, his 'breed side-kick, and the scum who ride with them. Not forgetting his boss, Mr Turner Lazenby.'

'Yeah, they're the boys, Miss Alicia,' said a surprised Floyd. 'How did you know?'

Poker Alice smiled. 'I've been able to read fellas' minds, fully dressed, or ballick naked, since fellas craved for me. I kept my eyes on you, Lazenby and Behen in the Prairie Dog last night. I could see that Lazenby and Mort Behen had a lot on their minds, especially Turner Lazenby, and they weren't joyful thoughts. And I also noticed that you were giving them more than just a casual eyeballin'. Bein' that Mort is a notorious bad-ass I figured that you could only be some sort of a lawman.' Poker Alice smiled again. 'You did right to come here, Mr Goad. As tough as you are you couldn't have kept up on your feet much longer. Now hang on in there for a few more minutes while I get someone to tend to that wound.'

Poker Alice hurried out of the room and to the head of the stairs. 'Otis!' she yelled. 'Get your big butt off that chair, *pronto*, and start earnin' your keep!' She waited till the bouncer, rubbing at his eyes, showed up at the foot of the stairs before she spoke again. 'Cock that scattergun of yours, Otis!' she called down. 'And if Mort Behen, his 'breed pardner, or any of his wild boys put as much as a foot on this front stoop, you blow them to hell, savvy?'

'Shoot them, boss?' a confused Otis said.

'Of course I mean shoot them, you dumb Swede,' Poker Alice snarled. 'Or by hell I'll turn that gun on you, and that's a promise!'

'You're the boss, Miss Alicia,' replied Otis. 'Shoot them it is.'

Poker Alice heard the bouncer click back the double hammers of the shotgun then move across the porch to stand guard at the door. Giving a satisfied grunt she walked along the corridor, past her own room to a door at the far end. She pushed it open and strode across to the bed and yanked back the sheet.

'Get your pants on, Doc, and bring your bag of tricks to my room,' she said. 'There's a man in there who needs urgent treatment for a bad knife wound, like yesterday. Or your wife gets to know that when you're away on an all-night call it ain't treatin' some rancher's family miles out of town.'

Doc Wallace, an elderly, grey-haired man, rolled sharply out of the bed and began putting his clothes on, fast. If Bertha, his sour-faced wife, president of the Church Meeting Society, found out that he regularly indulged in one of the sins of the flesh, by being entertained by lewd women, she would make his life more like Hell than she was doing already.

Poker Alice wasn't through with dishing out orders yet. 'Flo,' she said, to the doc's bed companion, 'you get some clothes on and go downstairs and boil up a pan of water, then bring it, and some clean cloths for bandages, to my room.' She slapped Flo's bare ass. 'Move, girl, move!'

Flo slipped out of bed as fast as Doc Wallace had. When Poker Alice spoke sharply, a girl did what she was told or Poker Alice would throw her out into the street and she would have to earn her living selling her favours as a two-dollar short-time girl in some dog-dirt saloon.

When Poker Alice returned to her own room, Floyd had slumped down in the chair, head on his chest. Poker Alice took in the dark, growing stain on Floyd's jacket. Her lips thinned in barely controlled anger. 'Damn your eyes, Lazenby!' she hissed. 'I hope you hang.' Her eyes were moist, which surprised her. Poker Alice thought, being that she had lived a hard and sinful life, she would never be able to shed tears of sympathy. The big dude had sure got her.

She opened a cabinet and took out a bottle of her special 'nightcap' brandy and filled out two glasses. She downed her drink in one. Then, gently raising Floyd's head, she put his glass to his lips. 'Get this down you, Mr Goad,' she said. 'The doc will be here in a minute or two. He ain't the most gentle of doctors, but he's an expert in treatin' gunshot and knife wounds. And don't worry about the 'breed coming here to make sure of you this time; one of my men is standing shotgun guard downstairs.'

Floyd opened his eyes and lifted his head and managed a smile at Poker Alice and sipped at the strong, belly-warming liquor. The doc couldn't hurt him any more than he was feeling right now. Dying would be a welcome relief.

Doc Wallace, shirt-tails flapping outside his pants, came into the room; his sleep-blurred vision clearing when he saw his patient.

'Mister,' he said, 'if you had to go and get a knife stuck in you, you couldn't have picked a better spot. And you were wise not to try and pull it out. You would have lost a whole bucket of your blood if you had.' He glanced at Poker Alice. 'Give him another slug of that medicine, Miss Alice, that knife's in deep.'

Doc Wallace ran his tongue over dry lips thirsting for the hair-of-the-dog. 'And I'd appreciate a measure myself, to kinda steady my hands.'

Poker Alice refilled her glass and handed it to the doctor, then she filled Floyd's glass again and held it while he drank. Doc Wallace, like Poker Alice, emptied his glass in one swallow then got to the business at hand. He rolled up his sleeves and took a pair of scissors out of his bag and began, carefully, cutting Floyd's coat and shirt close to the knife wound before removing them. Poker Alice, most unladylike, took a deep pull from the bottle of brandy when she saw the swollen purple edges of the wound, and the several white puckered skin scars of old wounds on his torso. She had to fight hard again to hold back her emotions. Doc Wallace would have a tale to tell in the Prairie Dog about Poker Alice bawling her eyes out over some wounded big dude. A lawman, she concluded, was someone special, born to the job. No ordinary man would be so crazy to get himself shot, knifed, whatever just for the pay that came with the badge. The big moon-faced son-of-a-bitch, Poker Alice thought, better pull through; he was a man she had a real craving to get to know more closely.

Flo came into the room with the hot water and a bundle of cloths hanging over her arm. 'Good,' said Poker Alice. 'Flo can stay here with you, Doc. If you want anything Flo will get it for you, OK? I'll stay till you get the knife out.'

Doc Wallace, intent on easing the blood-blackened pieces of cloth still sticking to the wound, only nodded.

Poker Alice shut her eyes and gripped Floyd's arm, pressing herself close to him as Doc Wallace took a grip of the knife handle. 'Now, this ain't going to hurt as much as it did when it went in, but it's in deep so it'll hurt some,' he said. 'But I don't mind hearin' a grow'd man hollerin' and a'cryin'. It kinda relieves his tension.'

Poker Alice's eyes once more dampened as she heard Floyd's deep shuddering groan as Doc Wallace eased the knife slowly out of the wound. And felt the dead weight of his body as it briefly fell against her.

'You weren't wrong, Doc,' Floyd said, feebly. With an effort he straightened up in his chair. He looked up at her with pain-washed eyes. 'I'm sure beholden to you, Miss Alicia, and you, Doc. I owe you a few drinks when I'm able to get around.'

'Yeah, I reckon you do, Mr Goad,' Poker Alice said. 'But try and not spill blood on my rugs the next time you call on me, and make it normal callin' hours.' She kissed

Floyd full on the lips. 'Now, I ain't got time to stand here and hold your hand as though you were some sick kid, tonight's business ain't over yet. Help him into my bed, Flo, when Doc's finished with him and look after him till I get back. And I won't forget that I owe you, Doc, for disturbing your night. Next time you come in, Flo will entertain you for free.'

Floyd's painful gasps as Doc Wallace bathed the wound while she was hurriedly dressing herself set Poker Alice's face into hard vengeful lines. By God, she thought, tonight's business was a long ways from being settled. Turner Lazenby was going to find that out. She saw that Floyd had mercifully passed out and Doc Wallace was deftly strapping bandages across his back. Doc Wallace looked up at her.

'He'll be OK, Poker Alice,' he said. 'He's a tough *hombre*. A little rest and he'll be strong enough to take another knife in his back.'

Poker Alice shot him a withering glance as

she left the room. Before stepping out on to the street she warned Otis to be on his guard. With Otis's sworn vow that no son-of-a-bitch would get past him ringing in her ears, Poker Alice, satisfied that she had done all she could concerning the safety of Mr Goad, walked briskly along the street to Silas Black's rooms. She hoped that the KP manager was a light sleeper, though she was prepared to wake up half the slumbering citizens of Abilene hammering on his door if he wasn't.

To her surprise she saw that Silas Black's office and rooms were a blaze of light and Silas Black and Marshal Blunt were standing outside on the boardwalk in deep conversation.

'Good Lord, Miss Alice!' Silas Black gasped on seeing her. 'What on earth are you doing walking the streets at this hour?'

Marshal Blunt touched his hat in greeting and gave her a polite, 'Evenin', Miss Alicia.' Then, thinking of the hot-blooded Big Kate, he added, 'Did Mr Goad tell you that I'd slung the Texan he brung in into a cell for a few days?'

'No, he didn't,' Poker Alice replied. 'He's–'

'Have you seen Floyd, Miss Alice?' interrupted Silas. 'That's who we are searching for. The livery barn owner got me out of bed to tell me that there had been a shooting at his place involving Mr Goad. Two men were killed and the barn owner swears that he saw a knife in Mr Goad's back. We're worried in case he's lying wounded someplace and passed out. The marshal's deputies are still out looking for him. Mr Goad's not a quack doctor, Miss Alice, he's a railroad agent, the best as well.'

'I already know that, Silas,' Poker Alice said. 'And he's OK. He's resting up in my private room. Doc Wallace is tendin' to his wound. The reason I was coming to haul you out of your bed, was that Floyd told me that the men who attacked him were some of Behen's gang. Pablo, the 'breed asshole, was the man who knifed him.'

'Thank God he's safe, Marshal,' a much

relieved Silas Black said. 'And thank you, Miss Alice, for taking him in. We know who's involved in the shoot-out, the barn owner told us. You and Floyd will be pleased to hear that the 'breed was also wounded in the fight.'

'As soon as Silas notified me of the trouble,' Marshal Blunt said, eager to keep in Poker Alice's good books, 'I deputized extra marshals and holding warrants for the arrest of the 'breed and Behen for attemptin' to murder a KP agent we went along to the freight yard. Once we got them behind bars then we could make a case against them as being the dynamiters. Silas reckoned that we should rope in Turner Lazenby as well. But we were too late. We found Lazenby shot dead in front of his looted safe, and Behen and his cutthroats have ass-kicked it out of town.'

'Well, you can pull your boys in now, Marshal,' Silas Black said. 'Now we know that Floyd is safe and well, and in good hands. Tell him I'll see him in the morning sometime to congratulate him on a job well done. The spur line can go through now without any more hitches.'

'I'll do that, Silas,' replied Poker Alice. She smiled at them both. 'I'll get back now and see if my patient needs any special attention. Goodnight, gents.'

Silas Black grinned at the marshal. 'I reckon a fella who's had a knife stuck in him, even a tough old goat like Floyd, isn't up to taking much of Miss Alice's special attention.'

'It could be one helluva nice way to go though, Silas,' the marshal said.

Fifteen

When Floyd woke up, the fiery pain in his shoulder had subdued to a dull nagging ache. He remembered Flo and Doc Wallace helping him to bed and taking off his boots and pants, then he must have passed out, or fallen asleep; whatever, it was time he was up and about. Not that he couldn't have stayed several more hours in Poker Alice's bed, the finest sprung bed he had ever slept in, relaxing under clean, sweet-smelling sheets, but he had an investigation to clear up. He reckoned by now Silas Black would know about the shooting at the livery barn and have taken measures to rope in Lazenby and Behen and his gang. Till they were all out of circulation the threat to the line still remained.

He slowly eased himself out of the bed,

trying to ignore the stabs of pain from his shoulder when he favoured his wounded arm, and sat on the edge of the bed and checked the secureness of the bandages. Doc Wallace had done a good job, they hadn't slipped at all. He reached across for his pants, lying over the back of the chair he had sat on while the doc had worked on him. He would need a shirt and a coat before he could leave the cathouse. Then he noticed that on a nearby armchair was a blanket and on one of the broad arms was a long-barrelled cavalry pistol.

Floyd smiled. Miss Alicia didn't do things by half helping out a man. On rare occasions he'd had women fuss over him, but not to the extent of being willing to throw down on any *hombre* intending him harm.

He was cursing and groaning, struggling one-handed to get his pants on when Poker Alice and Silas Black came into the room.

'Why are you outa that bed so soon, Mr Goad?' Poker Alice said, angrily. 'You'll open that damn wound and I told you I wanted no more blood spilt on my rugs!'

'I'll be OK, Miss Alicia,' Floyd said. 'Doc Wallace did a good job strappin' me up.' He glanced pointedly at the pistol on the chair. He grinned. 'And I'm too big for you to lose another night's beauty sleep on my behalf. I owe you for what you've done for me already.' Floyd's face hardened. 'Silas there could have tripped over my dead body in some alley, Miss Alicia, if you had turned me away. I take it you know why I'm here and that you've roped in Lazenby, Behen, and the rest of the dynamite gang, Silas.'

'The investigation hasn't been wrapped up as neatly as that, Floyd,' replied Silas. He then told Floyd about the killing of Lazenby and of Behen and his gang riding out of Abilene. 'Marshal Blunt thinks Behen will be heading for his old stamping grounds in Missouri to whoop it up with the cash he took out of Lazenby's safe. He's wired the law authorities across there to keep a sharp eye out for him. It makes no matter, Floyd.

We've, or I should say you, have got the sonsuvbitches off the KP's back, the new line should now go through on schedule. You've done a good job, Floyd; I'll say so in my report to the board.'

'Silas,' said Floyd, stone-faced, 'you help me on with my boots and find me a shirt and a coat. I've got to get out of here. I don't want to dampen your good feelin's about how successful my investigation's been.' He tapped his chest with a forefinger. 'But an old regulator's gut-feelin' is telling me that Behen ain't finished with us yet. He's maybe a mean, back-shootin' killer, but he ain't a man who runs scared when things go wrong for him. I figure him as a man who likes to win, or at least get even. He'll be lying low somewhere then hit the line while we're sittin' on our asses congratulatin' ourselves for a job well done.'

Silas Black close-eyed Floyd for a while before he spoke. If it came to a choice between Marshal Blunt's opinion and Floyd's gut-feelings regarding the whereabouts of Behen, and his possible next moves, he would accept as gospel truth Floyd's inner senses, hunches, or whatever he called them, on the matter.

'Then we must take further means to counteract that threat, Floyd,' he said, sober-faced. 'Stay at full alert along the line.'

Poker Alice gave a sarcastic laugh. With a voice more tinged with worry than anger she said, 'What further measures can you attempt, Mr Goad! If Behen sees your medicine wagon on the trail he'll blow it and you to hell and back. And you ain't fit enough to be bouncing up and down on a horse.'

Floyd couldn't meet Poker Alice's wild-eyed gaze. He knew she was right. His cover as a pill-pedlar, his only edge, was blown. And Ulysses would have to bend his knees like a camel for him to climb on to the saddle. And how could he face a shoot-out with a bunch of desperadoes with only one gun arm?

'Would you like me to quit my job, Miss Alicia?' he said, lamely.

Poker Alice gave him a cutting look. 'Quitting's better than being dead to most sensible fellas, Mr Goad,' she said. 'But I reckon a mule-headed *hombre* has to do what his stubborn mind tells him what he oughta do. I've got to go downstairs; I've got a business to run so I can't spend all morning jawin'. I'll leave it to you to work out which way you're goin' to die, Mr Goad. It's been nice to have made your acquaintance, short as it's been.' She cast Silas Black a sharp look. 'I'll see you at his funeral, Silas,' she snapped. She turned abruptly and all but ran out of the room. She didn't want to be angry with Floyd, she wanted to beg him to stay with her, but if the big man had a stubborn streak, so had she. It was better to cut him out of her life now than have to shed tears over him when he was brought back to Abilene, a tarp-wrapped bundle, strapped across his horse.

Silas Black smiled embarrassedly. 'She's

right you know, Floyd. I can bring in a bunch of Pinkertons to wind up the case. It won't take the shine off you; you did crack it, and you are wounded. No one will think of you as a quitter.'

'I know she's right,' Floyd said. 'And considerin' I'm beholden to her I've sure rubbed her up the wrong way. But I made a promise to the dead guards at the bridge that I would hunt down their killer and I ain't about to go back on my word given to men who died in the line of duty.' Floyd gave a painful shrug. 'And as Miss Alicia has so forcibly stated, even a dumb-ass has to honour a promise seriously given. Now give me a hand to get my boots on then you can get me a shirt and jacket and let me get outa here. I'd rather face Behen and the 'breed than suffer another tongue-lashin' from Miss Alicia.'

Sixteen

Beth watched Joshua talking to the man who had just ridden up to the house. The rider was speaking to Joshua without dismounting, and she noticed Joshua smiling. She guessed that he was being told when he was going to receive his reward money. Her pa had mentioned to her that Joshua was in line for a reward from the railroad for his part in preventing some outlaws from blowing up one of the bridges on the new line. She hadn't expected, indeed hoped, that Joshua would get his money so quickly, not wanting to lose his friendship this soon. Yet her pa had warned her that she had to be prepared for Joshua leaving the ranch.

'I ain't too happy myself that Joshua will be movin' on,' he had said. 'Bein' that I've only just hired him, and he's a good worker. But he's come into money and me, or you, ain't got the right to stand in his way if he wants to better himself. Bein' a hired man on a two-bit spread ain't a rewardin' future for a boy with money to contemplate.' Seeing her downcast look he had smiled at her. 'You're still young and purty, Beth, other boys will be ridin' this way to pay you a call, you'll see.'

'Not like Joshua!' she had snapped, and dashed back into her room, crying. She wished the railroad company would change their minds and not pay out the reward money.

Now it looked that her wish hadn't been granted, which, she thought, served her right for being so selfish. Joshua, as her pa had said, was entitled to live the life he wanted. She needed to ask him if he had got the reward, and if he was leaving the ranch. Instead, hiding her worries behind a sweet smile she said, 'Good news, Joshua?'

'Yeah, Beth,' replied Joshua, wide-faced

smiling. 'Two thousand dollars' worth; it's in the bank at Abilene. I can draw it out anytime I want! I'll be able to buy a section of land now!'

As casually as she could Beth said, 'Will that mean you'll be leaving us, Joshua?'

Joshua gave her a look of surprise. 'Leave you? What gave you that notion, Beth?'

'Well I thought ... well, Pa thought,' Beth said, 'once you got the reward money you'd want to build up a ranch, or a farm of your own, in Missouri, m'be.'

'Missouri?' said Joshua. 'There ain't anything for me in Missouri. Mr Spenser, the railroad superintendent, told me that the future of Kansas is in farming, not cattle. I'm takin' his advice by buyin' some land here in Kansas.' Po-faced he continued. 'The stretch of land beyond your home range. That's if my future pa-in-law don't object to runnin' a cattle ranch and a farm.'

'I don't know if my pa would want me to hitch up with a sodbuster, Mr Webb,' Beth replied, as straight-faced as Joshua.

A grinning Joshua took hold of her hand. 'We'll just have to go and see if he objects, Beth. If he does then he's lost himself a ranch hand.'

'Lost two, Joshua,' said Beth. Smiling she added, 'M'be three. Ma will be all for a wedding. She'll want to see her wedding dress being worn again.'

As he walked along the porch, arm around Beth's waist, Joshua suddenly remembered, what with the excitement of hearing about the reward money, and how it would affect his relationship with Beth, he had neglected to ask the rider if he had any news of Mr Goad. He would be in Abilene and he wondered how his hunting down of the dynamiters was progressing. He would invite him to the wedding; after all he had been responsible for getting him the reward. That's if the old goat was still in town and not prowling around the territory seeking out the men he was after.

Behen, before they had cleared the town limits, had decided where they would hole-up, the Carlson ranch. One man and two females wouldn't take much watching over, not if he impressed on the rancher that if he caused any trouble before he was ready to mount his next raid on the line he would end up a childless widower. And he had already made his mind up what section of line he would hit.

The bridge they had failed to destroy, he opined, would be too well guarded to risk attacking again, but south of the bridge the track ran along an earth and stone embankment for several hundred yards or so. Well-placed dynamite charges along the base of the bank would cause it to collapse and bring down the rails with it. Not only would it take weeks to rebuild but it should draw men from other parts of the track, weakening the defences all along the spur line, giving him the golden opportunity to hit the line hard and often, in true guerrilla fashion.

He glanced at the stone-faced Pablo riding alongside him, and reckoned that his mangled ear would remind the 'breed how he had been outsmarted till the day he died. He would be every bit as keen to keep up the fight against the railroad as he was. He favoured Pablo with a wolflike smile. 'We're headin' for the Carlson spread,' he said. 'I need you to throw a scare into his women-folk, enough to see that he don't cause us any grief for a few hours.'

Pablo, his part-ear burning like a flaming torch against the side of his head, was feeling just as painful mentally for the loss of face he had suffered at the livery barn. He would knife the whole Carlson family just to save the bother of standing guard over them and told Behen so.

'It may well come to that, Pablo,' replied Behen, 'if our backs are up agin a wall.' He hard-eyed the 'breed. 'Till then no one gets hurt, savvy? A lot of folk in Kansas think that the KP are land grabbin' sonsuvbitches and don't fret any at us raidin' them. Slit a coupla white women's throats and every man in the territory who can climb up on to a horse will grab his long gun and hunt us down. We ain't strong enough to take that kind of hassle, Pablo. And the rest of the boys wouldn't wear it; they ain't been paid to kill females.'

The train slowed down crossing the bridge, giving Floyd, who was standing on the first flatcar, time to professionally assess the bridge's defences. He saw a campfire in the wash with two men sitting at it, nearby were four tethered horses. The guards had been doubled. He nodded his head in a gesture of silent satisfaction, Silas Black had taken his warning to heart. As the train rattled its way to the rail-camp, he noted that extra guards had been posted on other vulnerable sections of the track. They both knew that the entire length of the line couldn't be made raid proof, but, Floyd opined, Silas was doing the best he could with the men he had available.

He himself was going to the rail-camp, along with six more men, to use it as a base. The train was also staying at the camp, the boiler at constant half pressure, ready to roll out with the six riflemen at any sudden alarm sent by the guards along the track via the Western Union telegraph wire that ran between Abilene and the camp. Again Floyd thought that it was the best they could do. It was better than having men scouring the territory looking for Behen and his gang. That could allow the sneaky bastard to slip by them and attack the line with impunity. It was watching and biting-nail time and Floyd could well understand Miss Alicia regarding him as a mule-headed crackpot. He smiled. What the hell, he thought, it was better than trying to sell quack cures, but only just.

As he attempted to clean out the big barn, Wade told himself angrily that trying to take in what Beth and Joshua had told him about getting married had allowed Behen and his gang to sneak up on him. If he had seen the sons-of-bitches approaching the ranch he would have easily held them at bay with the big Sharps.

After telling him the surprising news, Beth had gone back up to the house and Joshua had ridden off to the double bend in the creek to retrieve a calf that had strayed on to the open range on the other side of the water. Finishing his chore, mind still full of a forthcoming wedding, he had hurried to the house and seen how Meg was taking the news that she was getting a son-in-law, and found Behen and five men crowded together in the small parlour.

One of the men, a savage-faced part-Indian, wearing a bloodstained bandage around his head, had a big knife pressed against Beth's throat, forcing her head back. A white-faced Meg, hand at mouth, was being held by another one of the gang, and shot him a horrified look.

'I'll kill you, Behen, you sonuvabitch!' he

yelled, 'if that 'breed harms a hair on my girl's head!'

Behen laughed. 'You ain't in a position to do anything Carlson,' he said mockingly. 'There's no need for anyone to get hurt as long as you and your good lady carry on as usual about the place so that any rider passin' by on the trail will think all's normal here. We'll only be here a few hours.' Behen's face and voice steeled over. 'Try and sneak off to seek help and Pablo will take great pleasure in cuttin' your girl's throat, m'be cut off her purty hair as a souvenir.'

Somehow Wade held himself back from springing across the table and grabbing the 'breed by the throat and choking his evil life out of him. But it was Beth's, and Meg's lives at stake, he had to eat crow. His shoulders slumped, defeat written in his drawn, dead-eyed face.

'I'll do as you say, Behen,' he said, the words coming out as though it was hurting his mouth to say them. Cold-eyed he looked at Pablo. 'I know you, 'breed,' he said. 'Hurt her and I'll hunt you down and kill you, no matter how long it takes, and that's a promise. Come, Meg, let's see to the stock, before bein' in the same room as this scum makes me throw up.' He turned and walked out of the house.

Behind him, he heard Behen say, 'You can rustle up some chow for me and the boys, lady, before you feed the critters.'

You ain't holding all the aces, Behen, Wade thought, as he made his way to the barn. You don't know the kid is on the ranch. He hoped that Joshua, when he found out what was going on, wouldn't do anything foolish like barging into the house thinking that he could overpower six *pistoleros*. He believed Joshua wasn't a wild-headed glory-boy and would figure out some way to turn the tables on the gang. Wade knew that it was a slender hope but apart from a miracle happening it was the only hope he had.

Before he reached the creek Joshua saw the horses tethered in a hollow. Riding closer he counted six mounts, one of them wearing a fancy silver-worked saddle. The sight of the saddle rang warning bells in Joshua's ears. Mr Goad had mentioned to him that one of his chief suspects favoured such a rig. The gang must be in the house, jumped Mr Carlson before he had time to defend himself. What could be happening to Beth and her ma, made Joshua's blood boil over. He had to find out what was going on.

He dismounted and came on to the house in an elbow-and-knee-slithering crawl, and had to eat dirt when he saw three of the gang step out on to the porch. He cursed. There was no way now he could sneak up to the house and poke his gun through the window, cover the gang, and rescue the Carlsons. Frantic with worry, he tried to think of what he could do. If only Mr Goad were here, he told himself, he would know how to get the drop on six armed men. But the big lawman wasn't, so he would have to think up a plan of his own.

It was clear that he needed help, and the nearest place to the ranch to get that aid was at the rail-camp. He felt as though he was running out on the Carlsons, but staying here, wetting his pants with worry wouldn't help his future family any. He crawled back to his horse. With his back flinching, waiting for the shot that would tell him he had been seen, he rein-led it well away from the house before mounting and rib-kicking it along the trail to the line-camp.

Seventeen

Floyd was giving instructions to the extra guards he had brought with him when he saw the trail-dust of a horse being pushed to its full limit closing in on the camp. As the horse was yanked to a haunch-sliding halt he saw that its rider was Joshua. He also noted, by the kid's face, that he had a lot on his mind, all bad thoughts.

Joshua saw the big burly frame of Floyd. He wasn't on his own any more: he leapt out of his saddle and ran to him. 'That sonuvabitch, Behen and his gang are at Mr Carlson's ranch, Mr Goad!' he gasped out. 'They're holdin' the family captive! We've got to go and rescue them!'

'Calm down, kid,' Floyd said. 'How many men has Behen with him?'

'I counted six horses, Mr Goad,' replied

201

Joshua. 'So we'll need a big posse to take them on.'

Floyd rubbed his chin reflectively and, ignoring the wild-eyed Joshua, turned and spoke to Spenser who had come up alongside him. 'Behen and his boys are holed-up at the Carlson place, Phil. What's the nearest section of the line to the ranch that could cause you a whole heap of grief if blown up?'

'The trestle bridge you stopped the bastards from blowing up,' Phil said. 'But Behen, when he sees the extra guards there won't risk attacking it again.' Phil's face twisted in thought for a moment or two. 'Unless he....'

'Unless he what?' Floyd asked.

'There's a long embankment this side of the bridge,' Phil said. 'If that was destroyed hundreds of yards of track would collapse. It would take weeks of hard work to build it back up again.'

'Then we take it that the embankment's Behen's next target,' Floyd said. 'And I reckon he'll go for it tonight. He'll not want to stay too long at the Carlson place in case visitors call and see them.'

Joshua, face darkening in impatient anger, thinking of what could be happening to his bride-to-be, blurted out, 'Ain't you goin' to get some men mounted up, Mr Goad, and rescue the Carlsons?'

Floyd gave him a stern, fatherly look. 'These things can't be gone into lightly, Mr Webb. The Carlsons are safe for the present. Behen only wants to hole-up at their place till he's ready to hit the line again. Push him into a corner and he could turn vicious towards the Carlsons. It will be safer for them if we tackle the gang in the open.'

A scowling-faced Joshua accepted, grudgingly, the logic of Floyd's reasoning. After all, he thought, he was the expert.

'This is how we play it, Phil,' Floyd said. And in a few curt sentences gave the superintendent his orders.

'I'll see to that,' Spenser said. 'Good luck to us all. Let's hope we finish off Behen and his gang for good this time.'

Floyd cold-smiled. 'Let's hope we're right about Behen goin' for the embankment or our names will be mud. Now I'll get mounted up and ride out with the kid to the Carlson ranch before he starts a one-man rescue attempt.' He gave Joshua one of his beaming smiles. 'If I've been figurin' right, Mr Webb, Behen will be ready to pull out by now; we should find that the Carlsons are all OK.' Which wasn't necessarily true. Killers such as Behen and the knife-throwing 'breed were unstable characters, ready to wound or kill at a whim. Which wasn't news the kid would want to hear, he was worried enough already.

Joshua sat in his saddle in grim-faced silence. Floyd rode along still showing a confident, everything-will-be-OK face to Joshua. Inside he had the same inner worries as Joshua about the way things could be at the Carlson ranch. He also had a more personal worry. Something warm and sticky was coursing down his back, and it wasn't sweat. The jolting of riding had opened up his wound, and it was hurting like hell.

Below the last rise that led down to the ranch Floyd drew up his mount. 'We'll go in on foot from now on in, Mr Webb,' he said. 'And show me where they tethered their horses.'

Joshua saw Floyd ease himself slowly out of his saddle and wondered why he hadn't pulled out his long gun from its boot. Then for the first time he noticed the growing dark stain at Floyd's right shoulder, and the thickness of a bandage beneath his shirt. Good Lord, he thought, the old goat has been wounded. He had been too occupied with his own fears and worries to have asked Mr Goad how he had fared after he had left him at the Carlson ranch. And *he* supposed to be beholden to the big man.

'Your wound's bleedin', Mr Goad,' he said. 'How did you come by it?'

Floyd gave a strained grin. 'Me and the 'breed who rides with Behen kinda met up.

He stuck a knife in me. I evened things up somewhat by drawing a lot of blood on his face with a Colt shell.'

Joshua led him along the rim of the creek, keeping out of sight of anyone in the ranch house. He stopped, suddenly. 'The horses have gone, Mr Goad!' he exclaimed. 'But you can see where they were. Look!' He pointed to piles of horse droppings.

Floyd knelt down and picked up a dung ball. Indian fashion he held it to his cheek. 'Still warm,' he said. 'They ain't been gone long.' He had guessed right about Behen's plans, so far. The bastard intended hitting the line tonight. He prayed, for the kid's sake, that he would be right about the Carlsons being unharmed. He looked up for a comment from Joshua but he was already haring off to the house. With shoulder hunched up to hold in the pain he followed in his tracks. Before he reached the house, Joshua came rushing back on to the porch.

'The sonsuvbitches have taken Beth with them!' he cried.

Floyd's lips thinned in grim hard lines. He had only been part right and reckoned he deserved the accusing glare Joshua was giving him as he stepped past him to go into the house.

Wade Carlson was sitting in a chair, his wife bending over him washing the blood away from a nasty gash on his forehead. Floyd thought that the pair had aged twenty years since the last time he had seen them.

'They took Beth as a hostage, Mr Goad!' a fear-drawn faced Mrs Carlson said. 'It's to stop us raising the alarm when they left the ranch. Behen promised that she would be released unharmed when they've blown up the spur line.'

Wade Carlson tried to get up from the chair. 'Get my horse saddled up, Meg!' I ain't about to sit on my ass doin' damn all when my daughter's in those varmints' hands!' He groaned then sank back in the chair, unconscious.

'He's concussed,' Meg said. 'Behen struck him with his pistol when he tried to stop him from takin' Beth with them. He can't sit up on a horse.' She looked pleadingly at Floyd.

The Carlsons had been drawn unwittingly into what was strictly KP business, Floyd thought, and the railroad had to help them out. 'You keep Wade here, Mrs Carlson,' he said. 'Me and Joshua will bring Beth back. Grab the big Sharps, Joshua, we could have need of it. Let's go, we ain't far behind them!' Floyd hadn't just put on a brave show for Mrs Carlson's peace of mind. He believed that Behen didn't mean to hurt the girl, not out of the goodness of his heart, but the big trouble it would bring him if Beth was harmed. But she was a young pretty girl taken by men who took their pleasure the hard way.

It was Ulysses who warned them that it was time for caution. Floyd saw the big mule's floppy ears stiffen up and his hammer-head draw back to give out a neighing challenge. Floyd leant forward and cuffed him lightly on the nose. 'Keep quiet, you bone-headed sonuvabitch,' he said softly. 'I've got the message: there ain't no need to let the whole territory know.'

He gave a signal to Joshua to dismount, then, painfully, he dismounted himself. He hoped his wound wouldn't stiffen up, it was going to be two-gun work tonight. Leading their mounts, they pressed on, bright-eyed alert. At the edge of a stretch of brush they came on to the horses, six of them. Floyd grinned at Joshua. 'Ulysses weren't wrong,' he said.

Then he heard Joshua gasp, 'There's Beth!'

Through a gap in the brush Floyd saw Beth, hands and feet bound. Sitting several yards away from her was the 'breed. Joshua swung the Sharps up to his shoulder and took aim. Floyd spun round and knocked down the rifle with his pistol.

'What the heck…!' Joshua hissed angrily. 'I had a bead on him!'

'We're here to kill the bastards,' Floyd

grated. 'Not scare them off!'

'I don't give a hoot what happens to the gang, Mr Goad,' Joshua snarled back. 'I came for Beth!' He made to bring his rifle up again.

'Put that gun up to your shoulder, Mr Webb,' Floyd said, menacingly, 'and I'll pistol-whip you.'

Joshua took in the flinty-eyed look and slowly lowered the Sharps, though giving Floyd a fish-eyed look back. Floyd's gaze softened somewhat. 'I know it's upsetting seeing your girl in that bastard's clutches, but she ain't dead. Not like those two poor guards, or the railroad gang workin' at the cuttin'. One shot and Behen and his boys will scatter, even if they're on foot, we'll never catch them in this brush at night. And Behen could think that Wade Carlson had raised the alarm and go back to the ranch. Wade is in no state to protect himself, let alone his wife, is he?'

'But, Beth: we can't just leave her like that, Mr Goad,' Joshua said, the anger out of his voice now.

'I'll get Miss Beth back,' Floyd said. 'Silently.' He drew out a big knife from the inside pocket of his coat. 'But if things go wrong you have my permission to use the Sharps on the 'breed. Then you and the girl ass-kick it out of here fast, understand?'

Joshua was only half-listening to what Floyd was saying, he was thinking he was looking at the knife that had been in Mr Goad's back. The pain the big man must have suffered made his stomach heave.

Pablo's blood was running hot. Behen's orders that the girl had to stay alive to be used as a hostage, didn't stop him from having his way with her. He had time; it would take the boys at least another thirty minutes to lay all the charges. He got to his feet and walked across to her.

Beth had been worrying about her pa. She had heard him groan and collapse across the table, blood streaming from his brow from the pistol blow Behen had dealt him when he had tried to stop them from taking her with them. He could be dead, she thought fearfully, and couldn't hold back her tears any longer. Then she wondered where Joshua was. He must know by now what had happened to her. Was he riding to get help? Or coming to rescue her himself? She couldn't believe that he was running out on her, frightened. Yet she didn't want him to be killed on her behalf. She saw the look the 'breed was giving her as he walked towards her, loosening his belt. Her tears became deep body-shaking sobs. No one could help her now. Then, hardly believing her eyes, she saw Mr Goad standing behind her captor.

'Howdy, Pablo,' Floyd said. 'I've brung your knife back. Catch!' An underarm throw sent the knife flashing through the air.

Pablo, shock-faced, twisted round to catch the knife full in his chest. He stood swaying on legs that were unable to bear his weight before sinking slowly to his knees, hands clutching at the knife handle in a futile attempt to pull it out. Then he fell on to his face, limbs twitching in a final dying spasm.

Joshua came in running, dropped down at Beth's side and began cutting loose her bonds. When free, Beth clung to him tightly, sobbing out her relief. 'You're OK now, Beth,' he said, as he lifted her gently on to her feet.

'OK, you love birds,' Floyd said, smiling 'There's men's work to be done. You take one of the horses, Miss Beth, and make for home. Tell your pa to fort up in case things go wrong here.'

Beth firm-eyed Floyd. 'I can use a rifle, Mr Goad.'

'I know you can, Miss Beth,' replied Floyd. 'But your ma and pa will be worrying about you, so you ride off.'

Giving Joshua another hug and several kisses, Beth rode out, Joshua and Floyd much relieved to see her go. Now, Floyd thought, he could get down to the killing business, and he had the glimmering of a plan. The men he had told Spenser to send down the line by train would be in position now. They had orders not to fire on the gang till they heard firing from this side of the embankment, unless the dynamite charges were about to be lit. He had bet his reputation that the gang would be there, his gamble had paid off. They had the bastards ringed in and the chance to get them all.

'OK, Mr Webb,' he said. 'Get well out on to that left flank before you cut loose. I don't want you to get in too close to them, that's why I brought the big gun with us.' He grinned. 'It ain't any use rescuing Miss Beth then goin' getting' yourself shot, is it? You might spot one of the gang before you fire, but it don't matter. You just let them know you're here. The KP men's fire oughta send them scatterin' for their horses, and with only shells from a single-shot rifle to dodge, they'll think they've got it made.' Floyd gave another grin. 'I'll be blockin' that doorway, though not for the whole gang, I hope. So shoot true, Mr Webb.'

Joshua stretched out behind a slight rise

and keen-eyed the embankment for a target and picked out a dim figure moving along the track. Holding his breath he eased off a shot. The crack of the Sharps's discharge made his ears ring. He saw the man fold in the middle and drop out of sight. 'That bastard was for you, Beth,' he muttered, then thumbed in another load in the breech of the Sharps and joined in the firing that had burst out on the other side of the line.

Floyd drew back the hammers on both of the Colts and stood behind the horses, waiting. He had tightened the slip knots of the halter ropes so that they could not be easily jerked loose.

Behen ran along, dirty-mouthing. It was the second time he had led his boys into an ambush, and both of them laid by the KP agent. That fact chewed away painfully at his insides. He had managed to spring the first trap and though his luck was running bad again, it hadn't yet entirely deserted him. He still had the means, if he didn't get blown to hell by the big rifle, of showing the

KP son-of-a-bitch that he wasn't smart enough to box in an old Missouri brush boy. Pablo would be waiting with the horses, ready for a quick getaway. And he had the girl, his ticket to get out of the territory whole-skinned.

They had been almost ready to set off the charges on the embankment when he heard the sharp boom of a heavy calibre gun firing from the other side of the line. Then Saul, the look-out, came rolling down the grade with half his back blown away. The sudden burst of rifle fire from behind them downed two more of his boys. After that it had been a mad-assed scramble by him and Stu before they were part of the small massacre.

Suddenly Behen's confidence began to chill over. The KP agent had proved himself a smart operator so why was there only one single-shot rifle firing on this side of the track? The reason he came up with caused the chill to become real fear, reaching right down into him. His escape route was a death trail. Pablo, the girl, his life-saver, were no longer at the camp. He didn't have to guess who would be there to welcome him. Behen did some more swearing and hung back to let Stu get to the camp first to draw the shit away from him.

Floyd heard the rasping breathing of a man coming up to the horses, heard him cursing as he tried to loosen the knots of the tether ropes. He fired a load from both pistols and the man fell between the horses, vanishing from his sight beneath the kicking hooves of the gun-spooked horses. Behen heard the shots and stopped running. He bared his teeth in a death's head grin. The KP agent had played his last sneaky trick. In a light-footed gait he ran to his right to come on to the horses from the rear.

The shooting had ceased beyond the embankment and Floyd couldn't hear any sounds of men haring through the brush. Had all the gang been killed? Only after a body count would he be certain that the Behen gang was no more. Like Behen, for no apparent reason, Floyd's sixth-sense began to play up. He knew he was getting old, and being wounded and all, but that wasn't setting his nerves on edge. Behen was still alive, skulking out there in the dark, the cunning bastard had smelt out his trap. The hunted had become the hunter. Floyd began to sweat.

He shifted his ground slowly, getting nearer to the darker background of the horses. In the rapidly growing darkness, Behen would have to get close in before he could fire a killing shot with certainty. Close enough, he hoped for him to hear his approach, and show him from which direction the attack would come. He would have to depend on his reactions when Behen made his play, and they were anything but quick right now. It was Ulysses who gave him back his lost edge.

He heard the mule's bad-tempered snort; Behen was coming in at his back. 'Ulysses,' he breathed, 'you should be the regulator.' He tightened his grip on his pistols and waited for a few nerve-jangling seconds, then spun round, firing the Colts in one non-stop sweeping burst into the brush in front of him. Through the gunfire smoke-haze, Floyd thought he saw one answering gun flash from the brush.

Three of the shots had caught Behen low down, his confident grin vanishing in a paroxysm of pain. His dying reflexes fired off one wild shot as he collapsed in a writhing and screaming heap.

Floyd's hair rose at the nape of his neck at the blood-freezing sounds of a man dying hard. He held his guns on the brush till the screams died away to a hoarse gurgling moan, then like the thrashing of limbs had, they died away altogether. It was only then he was conscious of a knife-slash-like pain on his right thigh. Behen had paused long enough on his way to Hell to put a slug in him.

Floyd's body sagged wearily, his gasp of relief came out long and loud. It was high time he was quitting the regulating business, he thought. He put his guns away, too played out to reload them.

'Are you OK, Mr Goad?' he heard Joshua call out. 'I heard you shootin'.'

'Yeah, I'm OK,' he replied as Joshua came up to him. 'I think I've downed Behen. He's lyin' in that bush there. He ain't stirred since I practically pumped two full loads in his direction. The sonuvabitch was tryin' to Injun-up on me. Bein' that we can't hear any more movin' about I reckon that between us and the KP guards we've wiped out the whole gang.'

'I got one of them myself,' Joshua said, proudly.

'Good,' said Floyd. He didn't tell Joshua he had been wounded in the leg. The kid had played his part well for the KP, it was long past time he got to living his own life again. 'It's all over for you here, Joshua,' he said. 'You get back to that girl of yours before she comes ridin' back here to see if you're OK.' He shook Joshua's hand. 'We couldn't have seen this business cleared up without your help, but don't get a hankerin' for it. Stick to ranchin'; this kind of work ain't worth a light.'

'You sure you'll be OK if I ride out, Mr Goad?' Joshua asked. 'You sure don't look so good what with your wound openin' up and all.'

'Yeah, I'm fine,' Floyd replied, wanting the kid to go before he passed out; then he would feel obliged to stay with him. 'Now vamoose when I tell you to; the KP boys will be this way soon, they'll see to me. Before you go can you oblige me by firin' three shots in the air to let them know that the fightin's over.'

Joshua mounted up after he had heard the replying three shots from the other side of the line. He was about to dig his heels in his horse's ribs when he thought that it was only right and proper to tell Floyd his good news.

'Me and Beth Carlson are goin' to get hitched, Mr Goad,' he said. 'You'll be invited to the weddin', if you're still in the territory that is.'

'Thanks, Mr Webb,' replied Floyd. 'I'll be there. I wouldn't miss the chance to have a kiss at such a purty bride. I could be bringing a lady friend, if that's OK by you.'

'That's fine by me, Mr Goad,' a surprised Joshua said. He didn't reckon the big man had been long enough in Abilene to strike up a relationship with a female. The old goat must be as fast roping in females as he was shooting down bad-asses. He favoured Floyd with a curious look. 'I didn't know you had a lady friend in town, Mr Goad?'

Floyd smiled. 'The lady in question don't know she's my friend yet, Mr Webb.'

Joshua came out with a loud, 'Well I'll be durned!' and burst out laughing. 'I'm ridin' out,' he said, 'before you surprise me any more. I'll get word to you when the weddin's comin' off, pardner.' Then he let his horse have its head.

Poker Alice held in her feelings when she opened her door and found Floyd standing there. She took in the haggard, unshaven-

face, his ripped trouser leg, showing another dirty wound bandage, and guessed, by the way he was hunched up, his shoulder wound was troubling him. She wanted to burst into tears and hug him on seeing the state he was in. She also felt like telling him he had heaped all the pain on himself for following such a dangerous profession. He was damn lucky to be still alive.

Instead she said, shut-faced, 'You sure know how to dress up, Mr Floyd T. Goad, when callin' on a lady.'

'Things have been kinda hectic lately for me to get dressed up formal-like, Miss Alicia,' replied Floyd. 'I was hopin' you could put me up for a spell, m'be till my ex-pardner gets himself married.' Floyd's big ear-to-ear smile lit up his bloodless face. 'I intend escortin' you to that joyous occasion, Miss Alicia, if I ain't takin' a liberty askin' you.'

'Come on in, you big ape, and I'll clean you up,' Poker Alice said. 'What the hell's a few blood-stained rugs amongst friends?

You'll give my place a bad name standing there like some saddle-bum. And I'll be delighted to come with you to that weddin'. Someone has to keep you from gettin' stabbed or shot again, haven't they, Mr Floyd T. Goad?' Then her stoic-mask slipped as she burst into tears of happiness as she reached out her hands to Floyd.